Windswept

PROMISE

ENDORSEMENTS

I absolutely loved reading Windswept Promise! It's such a captivating story that had me hooked from beginning to end. Every character is brought to life with such detail that I felt like I knew them personally. I couldn't put the novel down—just had to know what happened next!
—**Marienne Wood**, age 13

An intriguing journey from the Gulf coast to the sweeping plains of Texas. Visual adventures and resounding sounds abound from Tim's skillful use of words. His characters reflect sorrow, hope, fear, courage, and determination—all fulfilled with the spirit of faith and love.
—**Mary Berry**, retired teacher, Christian friend and neighbor

I love the way Tim intertwines history and fiction into his writing. Besides being entertaining, Windswept Promise is extremely well written. I can't wait to read the sequel!
—**Susie Culver**, Houston, Texas

Hold on to the reins! You are about to embark upon a cross-country adventure from a Catholic orphanage to the Wild, Wild, West. Laurabeth goes on a hunt for her Uncle "Useless" whom she didn't know existed. Oh, the people you'll encounter along the way. A fun read at any age. Tim has an innate talent for drawing you into the story. Can't wait for his next book!
—**Deb Jacklin**, Morris, Illinois

Tim Lewis has brought the Wild West of 1887 back to life with his vivid characters, and story of family bonds and feminine willpower. Trains, buggies, cowboys and villains make this an adventure for both characters and readers. I hope all of my grandchildren will read this book and relive the history of private freighting on the Texas Plains. It will make them appreciate Amazon!

—Julie Mitchell, Amarillo, Texas

I thoroughly enjoyed reading Windswept Promise! The authentic main character "connections" concerning the joys and rigors of ranch life atop the Texas High Plains kept me turning pages from beginning to end.

—Carolyn Sherrod, Canyon, Texas

A brave young lady, a cowboy, and a mystical wild stallion. Who can resist? Windswept Promise tells the story of young Laurabeth Appleby, who undergoes a perilous journey from Galveston to the Texas Panhandle in 1887. She's not only searching for a long lost uncle, but a future of love and happiness. The evil plotting of a dastardly villain offers plenty of danger and suspense. While the famous XIT Ranch—with its cowboys, horses and kooky characters—provides a colorful and realistic backdrop in this exciting western adventure. Mr. Lewis' talented storytelling will have the readers turning pages to the end!

—Nancy Slover, Christian writer and Poet, San Marcos, Texas

Windswept PROMISE

Timothy Lewis

ELK LAKE PUBLISHING INC.

PUBLISHING THE POSITIVE
Plymouth, Massachusetts

A Christian Company
ElkLakePublishingInc.com

COPYRIGHT NOTICE

Cover: Kelly Artieri, Derinda Babcock
Interior Design: Deb Haggerty
Editor(s): Cristel Phelps, Deb Haggerty

PUBLISHED BY: Elk Lake Publishing, Inc., 35 Dogwood Drive, Plymouth, MA 02360, 2024

Library Cataloging Data
Names: Lewis, Timothy (Timothy Lewis)
Windswept Promise / Timothy, Lewis
202p. 23cm × 15cm (9in × 6 in.)
ISBN-13: 9798891341357 (paperback) | 798891341364 (trade paperback) | 798891341371 (e-book)
Key Words: Christian Faith; Young Adult; Historical Romance; Western Adventure; Texas Frontier; Pioneer Ranching; Horses and Wagons)
Library of Congress Control Number: 2024xxxxxx Fiction

DEDICATION

To Lana and Billy,
Shooting stars both!

ACKNOWLEDGMENTS

Thank you to my good friend and mentor, Dr. Garry L. Nall, who initially edited, then urged me to publish "Freighting on the XIT Ranch of Texas" in the *Panhandle-Plains Historical Review*. The article became the primary building blocks for *Windswept Promise*.

Also, thanks to Deb, Cristel, Derinda, Kelly, and the rest of the talented publishing team at Elk Lake. Your friendship, expertise and professionalism allow me to share the faith stories that brew inside my mind and heart.

And to my wife, Dinah, who travels with me daily—over the horizon.

Finally, praise be to God, the Author of us all!

CHAPTER 1

MAY 18, 1887
GALVESTON, TEXAS

Laurabeth Appleby smoothed her dress and faced the heavy wooden door—alone. She drew in a deep breath and released it, hating how her hands perspired.

Perhaps the Reverend Mother was napping?

Gathering courage, she knocked softly, then squeezed her clammy fingers and waited for a reply.

"Come in, child."

Tiptoeing from the stuffy hallway, Laurabeth entered the breezy sitting room. She'd visited Mother Ruth O'Brien's private quarters twice. First, the sultry September day her father brought her to stay *temporarily* at the orphanage by the sea. Second, a month later when his ship went down. Over two years had passed, and here she stood again.

Her stomach tightened. What new tragedy awaited?

"Please, sit." Positioned in a highbacked rocker, Mother Ruth gestured toward a worn, velvet couch—the last place Laurabeth sat beside her father.

"I trust you've had a pleasant birthday?"

"Yes, Reverend Mother. Sister Martha baked a cake, and the children made presents."

"Excellent. And the necklace?"

"From Sister Mary Michael." Laurabeth glanced at the string of tiny pink and white seashells. "Eighteen. One for each year of my life."

Mother Ruth smiled as the salty air ruffled her black habit. "I see. The age a girl becomes a woman."

The statement was no secret. Upon turning eighteen, children were encouraged to leave the orphanage and make their own way. Schooled in basic trade skills, boys found jobs. Girls either married or answered the call to lifetime religious service. Laurabeth felt no calling to be a nun. Surely the kind Sisters of the Incarnate Word wouldn't push her out onto the street, nor expect her to wed the first man who came along.

The Reverend Mother stood, then paused before stepping to a polished oak writing desk in front of a double window. Stripes of late afternoon sunlight filtered through slatted storm shutters. From beneath a stack of papers, she produced a small, sealed envelope. "I pray giving you this letter today is wise."

Laurabeth's mouth flew open, yet she was too stunned to speak. The only people she knew lived at the orphanage. If the letter was a birthday gift, who sent it? What sort of present might be unwise?

The envelope felt heavier than Laurabeth anticipated. She scanned the address:

Miss Laurabeth Appleby
St. Mary's Orphan Asylum
Galveston, Texas

There was no return address, stamp, or postmark.

She gasped. A familiar hand had scribbled her name.

"Papa's handwriting." Laurabeth's heart pounded. "Is he alive?"

"No, child." Mother Ruth sat on the couch. "This envelope was inside a larger one addressed to me. The package arrived by courier the day your father sailed. Inside was a generous gift to the Asylum." She paused and placed a gentle hand on Laurabeth's shoulder. "Captain Appleby requested that if he didn't return, I was to present this letter to you. Today."

Laurabeth wanted to laugh and cry at the same time. Her arms trembled. Hadn't she experienced enough anguish? Mama died of yellow fever. Papa's ship sank in a hurricane. However, an unread letter was like having him back for a brief, special moment. Carefully tearing open one end, she slid out the contents. Inside were several folded pieces of white parchment and a twenty-dollar gold piece.

"That's quite a present." Mother Ruth smiled. "Do you wish to be alone to read your father's words?"

Wagging her head, Laurabeth unfolded the thin sheets. Printed at the top of each page was his standard business letterhead, beginning with the ship he'd named after her mother.

THE LADY ELIZABETH
WORLD-WIDE TRADE in COTTON and COFFEE
(Owner/Captain—Jonathan Appleby)

Laurabeth read the salutation, the same four words he'd penned countless times.

My dear sweet Laurabeth,

A tear rolled down her cheek, splatting onto the paper. She shivered.

Mother Ruth reached for the letter. "Shall I read aloud?"

Laurabeth nodded, burying her face in her hands.

> My dear sweet Laurabeth,
> Happy Birthday! I'm sure you've grown more beautiful than I could imagine. By now, you know I've stepped across the narrow barrier separating life from death to join your precious mother in glory. Remember how much we both still love you.

Mother Ruth cleared her throat. "Continue?"

Again, Laurabeth nodded. As long as she wasn't required to speak, her tears remained on the inside. When Papa vanished, she'd wept for days. Afterward, she'd vowed to be in command of her emotions around others.

> As a gentleman—and most significantly, your father—duty commands I confess you still have family. An uncle. My brother, Eustus Appleby.

"Papa has a brother?" The response blurted from her lips.

The Reverend Mother paused, squeezed Laurabeth's shoulder and continued.

> To my knowledge, he never married. Last month, I met a man who'd made acquaintance with a Eustus Appleby residing in Fort Worth, Texas, at Dawson's Boarding House. Mister Appleby—a bachelor—said he was raised in Pendleton County, Virginia, near the settlement of Honey Grove. Unless I'm mistaken, this gentleman must be my brother, Eustus.

Laurabeth's head spun. Papa never mentioned a brother. She scurried to the double window and peered outside. Perhaps the vast expanse of sand and waves would work their calming magic. "Reverend Mother, please go on."

> Understand, sweet child, to forever conceal this information wasn't my desire. I had no idea of my

brother's whereabouts and little way of finding him. Yet, after the recent news of his location, I determined to journey to Fort Worth and inquire of his situation with utmost diligence. Perhaps Eustus would consider forgiving me since the passing of years has helped fade the bitter conflict.

"What bitter conflict?" Laurabeth whirled biting words back toward the couch. "Why does my Papa need forgiveness?"

"I don't know, child." Mother Ruth's soft gray eyes exhibited their own calming effect. "None of us possess the mind of God."

"I'm sorry, Reverend Mother. Please continue."

Therefore, lovely daughter, today you are of age to make your own pilgrimage in search of the uncle you know not, if meeting him is your desire. The gold piece is more than enough for lodging and roundtrip train fare to Fort Worth. In closing—

"How old is my uncle?" Laurabeth's face muscles tightened. "How will I recognize him? What if I go there and he refuses to see me?"

Mother Ruth chuckled. "Why not write to him first?"

Laurabeth faced the window, her breathing shallow. She'd not been off Galveston Island since coming to the orphanage. Fort Worth was a reckless cowtown on the edge of the Texas frontier.

"Sit, child. This isn't easy news."

"I'm fine, Reverend Mother. Please finish."

In closing, I hope time spent with the benevolent sisters has eased your pain. On the date of this reading, you'll legally inherit the Appleby estate. I've instructed it be sold at fair market value. My attorney, Mr. Bowman, will contact you and handle all banking and investment details. The annual monies received shall provide a comfortable living wherever you wish to settle.

Until we hug at heaven's gate.

All my love,

Papa

Tears pooled in Laurabeth's eyes. Before her father's last voyage, they agreed if he perished, she'd not live alone at the Appleby estate but reside at the orphanage.

The sitting room walls closed in.

Her legs weakened.

"The fire. Papa never knew about—" She swallowed. "His plans for me are ruined."

Mother Ruth stood. "Calm yourself, child. You know you may remain here."

"Papa never saw the horrible flames."

"Which are six months past. There's no need to worry."

Laurabeth pictured the deadly orange glow hovering over Galveston. Felt the intense inferno that devoured the Appleby home, plus five hundred others.

"You may live at St. Mary's as long as you need." Mother Ruth's voice was steady. She placed her arms around Laurabeth. "There's no cause for fear. God takes care of his children."

Breaking free, Laurabeth flung open the sitting room door, bolted down the hallway and out the main entrance. Thoughts of the thick, black smoke suffocated Mother Ruth's brave words.

Laurabeth had to get to the beach to breathe.

Needed room to think.

A place to cry.

Sprinting past a bushy growth of salt cedar, she faced the stiff ocean breeze, pausing to unlace her shoes and remove her stockings. A single tear fell, then another.

Barefoot, she crossed the rippled sand dunes as a sudden rush of emotion burned her eyes. And then her toes felt the squish of wet sand, the splash of warm surf.

She stopped.

Soft foam wet the hem of her dress, bubbling around her ankles and calves before rushing out beneath her feet. A seagull swooped low with a lonesome cry. On the western horizon floated the golden ball of sun, its rays painting crimson and pink on a canvas of wispy white clouds. In front of her spread the endless Gulf of Mexico.

Why, Heavenly Father, is everything in my life a broken promise?

"Mama vowed not to catch the fever. Papa swore he'd come home."

Her wails met the constant rhythms of sea air and water.

"And the fire. The fire destroyed … Oh—"

A breaking wave slapped Laurabeth's knees. Losing balance, she plopped on her bottom into the salty water, drenching her dress and long, flaxen curls.

Now reclining on both elbows, Laurabeth allowed her legs to float in the comforting surf.

Oh, Lord, I'm like the wind-driven waves, tossed about by one tragedy after another. Is this my destiny? Where's the happiness?

"Out of my way, birthday girl." A blur of black robe and burgundy cincher splashed into waist-deep water, then dove underneath.

Laurabeth giggled. Sister Mary Michael was hilarious, especially with a soaked habit.

The nun surfaced. "So, Shorty. Sneaked out here to swim without me when I have a second birthday gift."

"Another?"

Mary Michael stood and nodded.

"But this one's perfect." Laurabeth sat upright and placed a hand on her neck.

Good. The necklace is still there.

"If you adore that old thing, wait 'til you see this." Sister Mary Michael inched closer.

"What?"

"Guess."

"Give me a hint."

"Your next gift is hidden behind my back."

Laurabeth frowned. "Give me a color."

The dripping nun waddled closer. "Light brown, like your eyes."

"Something to wear?"

"Of course." Mary Michael stepped forward and heaved a double handful of wet sand into Laurabeth's lap. "Surprise."

The girls chased each other along the deserted beach until breathless, stopping to rest on a large piece of driftwood. This time, tears of laughter wet Laurabeth's eyes. "Did the Reverend Mother send you to cheer me?"

"Worked, didn't it?"

Laurabeth grinned. Mary Michael brightened any dull mood. The nun was only three years older yet possessed a deep level of understanding. Perhaps because she too was orphaned.

"Have you ever had a wish *almost* come true?" Laurabeth attempted to uncover a penny-sized sand crab with her big toe.

"Almost?"

"I mean, you hope and pray, believing with all your heart an event will happen. Instead, something else occurs. A circumstance you never dreamed."

"Around here, we call that *faith*." Mary Michael uncovered the shattered piece of a paper-thin shell.

"Another broken angel wing. I wonder why I keep digging these up."

"'Cause one day you have *faith* you'll find a whole one."

"Exactly." The older girl grinned. "And so will you."

Laurabeth threw her arms around her friend. Mary Michael always knew.

Always understood.

In the distance, the supper bell rang.

The nun leaped to her feet. "Oh no. I'm late for kitchen duty. Sister Martha will have my hide."

"That's nothing new."

Mary Michael was already headed up the beach. "Let's get your dress washed and hung out tonight," she shouted. "I'll hold you a plate. You're too skinny to skip meals."

Laurabeth watched her friend fade into the shadows, then gazed across the Gulf's dusky expanse. Soon, the moon would rise, its silver path glistening across the waves. She drew in a deep breath and released it.

Her mind was clear.

Although leaving Sister Mary Michael and the safety of the orphanage was daunting, she'd buy a ticket the next morning and board the train to Fort Worth. Locating the uncle she'd never met was risky, yet key, in forging her future.

Laurabeth smiled.

Most of all, she desired the same feeling of contentment from when her folks were alive.

Genuine happiness.

Finding it ... a self-made promise.

Her journey north was the first step.

CHAPTER 2

Clocktowers across Galveston chimed four p.m. At a quarter past, Laurabeth and Sister Mary Michael pushed their way onto the crowded wooden platform at the Gulf, Colorado, and Santa Fe Depot.

Marching alongside the waiting train, a conductor wearing eyeglasses and a crisp black uniform paused to retrieve a pocket watch attached to a thin gold chain. He popped open the shiny cover. "All aboard!"

"I wish I could keep this safe with me." Laurabeth balanced a small trunk atop a piled luggage cart. "Compared to most travel cases, mine doesn't require much room."

Sister Mary Michael grinned. "After the case survived a hurricane, I wouldn't worry too much about the perils inside a baggage car."

Laurabeth adjusted the blue fabric bow attached to her round straw hat, then sighed as she watched her most valued possession wheeled away to be loaded—Papa's sea chest with the initials J.A. embossed on the brass latch. Floating amongst the wreckage of the *Lady Elizabeth*, the chest was discovered after the storm by a passing frigate. Only his favorite pipe remained inside. Now the contents included Laurabeth's few clothes plus the three items she'd saved from the horrible fire—the same pipe, the family Bible, and her mother's wedding gown.

"All aboard!"

"Wait," Mary Michael said. "I have another gift."

"More wet sand?"

From a shopping bag she carried, the nun produced a wicker basket draped with a red and white checkered cloth. "Sister Martha baked her tasty buttermilk biscuits, and we added a jar of cane syrup. I wanted to sneak a jar of mayhaw jelly, but—"

"Oh, Mary Michael." Laurabeth flung her arms around her best friend. "You take such good care of me. I won't have to buy all my food."

"Careful," she warned, then cackled. "You don't want crumbled biscuits stuck to your clean dress ... after we stayed up half the night washing and ironing."

"All aboard!"

The massive locomotive hissed, spewing a cloud of steam onto the platform.

"Do you still have your ticket and money?"

Stooping briefly, Laurabeth felt for the hidden pocket they'd sewn underneath the skirt of her duel-piece calico print, just above the hem. Before she could answer, the railcar chain jerked into motion with two short whistle blasts. She stood upright, her eyes misty.

"I'd best get a letter from Fort Worth." Mary Michael flipped up a curl of Laurabeth's hair and twirled it around a finger before letting it drop.

A jumble of words caught inside Laurabeth's throat as she backed toward the moving train. Was she seeing Mary Michael's mischievous eyes for the final time? Hearing her comical laugh?

The conductor's firm hand grabbed Laurabeth's sleeved arm from behind, pulling her onto the rear steps of the last passenger coach. "In the future, miss," he scolded, "I'd be more mindful when boarding."

Too embarrassed to reply, she nodded and hurried inside. The railcar's rocking motion made walking difficult, but Laurabeth managed to drop into one of the few empty benches midway up the aisle. Nearby sat two children. The rest of the passengers were adults.

Scooting to the open window, she peered outside. The depot and Sister Mary Michael had disappeared from sight.

Laurabeth sighed. Her nightlong journey had finally begun.

The train picked up speed, huffing across the narrow bay bridge toward the mainland. She removed her hat. Windblown hair was a comfort, reminding her of one of Papa's silly rhymes.

Most lovely of messes
(This seaman confesses)
Are wind-tattered tresses
Adorning fine dresses.

She smiled at the memory. He loved to surprise his wife and daughter with expensive gowns, many purchased halfway around the world.

Laurabeth dug her ticket from the hidden pocket, then gazed out over the choppy water. Behind stood Texas's most modern city. Located on an island, some considered Galveston a paradise atop a mile-wide sandbar. To her—a place where joy melted into one nightmare after another.

She swallowed.

Ahead lay a rough cowtown on the edge of civilization.

Will my Uncle Eustus be there?

The thought made her shiver, her mouth dry. When boarding, she'd noticed the necessary room. Outside the door was a bucket of drinking water with a tin dipper. Perhaps a cool sip would—

"Your ticket, Miss." The conductor waited beside her bench. He gestured toward her hands. "Your ticket?"

"Oh, yes."

He collected her ticket and continued to the next passenger. Before he moved to the next car, the train crossed onto the mainland.

Tiny pieces of soot rode atop the humid coastal breeze, floating through every open window. Farmhouses adorned with tin-roofed barns and herds of grazing livestock dotted the level countryside. A distant mule team pulled a machine cutting hay.

Laurabeth settled into her seat, allowing the open spaces to perform their magic.

She studied her immediate surroundings. The railcar had once been a fine coach. Much of the brass ornamentation was missing, likely reinstalled in the plush diners and Pullmans of newer express trains. The upholstered benches remained intact. However, the seat ahead was torn and unoccupied.

Hearing the rasp of shuffling cards and the jingle of coins, Laurabeth turned to see a group of men huddled in the rear of the car playing poker. Facing front, her cheeks warmed. A player wearing a smudged green derby watched. She'd briefly caught his stare, felt the penetration of cold, dark eyes.

Laurabeth shivered.

Why would a stranger gaze so intently? Perhaps he'd worked for her father. Pivoting her head, she forced another glance. He tipped his hat. His lips split into a sly smile. She slumped low in her seat and focused on the passing scenery.

Clumps of tall pines dotted green pastures, their pencil thin shadows crisscrossing in the late afternoon sunlight. Miniature grass-covered hills resembled carpeted sand dunes draped in patches of brilliant wildflowers. Stands of bluebonnets blended with orange Indian paintbrush and crimson sweet clover. She breathed in the delicate inland scents and closed her eyes. The stranger was soon forgotten.

The train slowed with a jerk. Laurabeth caught herself dozing, so sat upright, expecting to see the outskirts of a town. Instead, a middle-aged couple ran alongside the train. Dressed in bib overalls and a felt hat, the man lugged a large burlap bag. The woman wore a gingham dress with matching sunbonnet.

Laurabeth leaned her head out of the window.

Can't they wait for the train to stop?

In an instant, the woman gathered her skirts and leaped toward the moving coach.

"Watch out," Laurabeth screeched.

The conductor's arm shot out from the rear steps, assisting the woman. The man pitched on his bag, grabbed the handrail, and swung himself up.

The poker players laughed.

Ducking back inside, Laurabeth wanted to crawl beneath her bench and remain there forever. How was she to know proper boarding procedure when there was no train station.

"Excuse me, miss, but is this bench taken?"

"Um ... no ... sir." Laurabeth was embarrassed to be located behind the only vacant seat. Maybe the couple who'd just boarded would ignore her.

The man removed his sweat-stained felt, allowing the woman to sit first. "We're Chester and Lawanda Peacock from over near Sandy Point."

"Laurabeth Appleby."

"Don't recall ever meeting no Applebys." Chester grinned "But we don't travel much. Have to flag down the locomotive." He sat beside his wife, then cocked his head toward Laurabeth. "Are you coming or going?"

"Chester honey, don't be nosey. Ain't none of our business." Lawanda glanced back and smiled. "We're headed up to Temple. Our youngest son is getting married."

"Congratulations." Laurabeth heard the poker players snicker. Perhaps their gleeful mood concerned something else.

"'Bout time that boy got hitched," Chester said. "If a man's gonna be successful in life, he needs the constant loving of a good woman."

"Chester." Lawanda blushed.

He continued. "A man and woman got to meet each other's needs. Work together as a team. Two mules can plow twice as far as one."

Lawanda offered her husband a playful punch. "This ain't the time nor place to talk romantic. Let's not bore this young lady any longer."

Chester and Lawanda faced forward.

"It's nice meeting you." Laurabeth never considered the idea, but her parents had worked as a team, sailing around the globe together. While her father attended to Captain's duties, her mother oversaw the galley and kept the books. After Laurabeth came along, the three of them traveled to England and the Caribbean Islands. When they weren't at sea, Papa shared the home chores. Then, Mama died of the fever, and he became overprotective. That's why Laurabeth stayed at St. Mary's Orphan Asylum during his final voyage. Located away from the city, the orphanage was thought to be less affected by disease.

The passengers were quiet, except for faint chuckles from the poker game. As dusk settled upon the passing landscape, Laurabeth fixed her gaze upon the couple seated ahead. Chester stretched out his arm, while Lawanda relaxed in the crook of his elbow. They seemed happy. Perhaps one day, Laurabeth would meet a man who'd love her, and they too would be a team. A tingle leap-frogged up her spine.

"Next stop, Richmond." The conductor's shout startled Laurabeth from her thoughts. He entered the car and lit a gas lamp. "Thirty-minute stop to take on water."

The train soon squealed to a halt. Lawanda stood. "Miss Appleby? We're gonna hunt up a quick bite to eat. You're welcome to tag along."

"That's very kind, but I've brought my supper." Laurabeth gestured toward her basket. "I've enough to share."

Chester winked. "Much obliged, young lady. Maybe next time. I've been promising the wife a meal out. A restaurant here serves up the tastiest barbecue within a hundred miles. We'd best hurry."

The Peacocks, along with the other passengers bustled off to find something to eat. Cool night air streamed into the empty coach carrying rhythmical calls from station vendors, and the smoky aroma of roasted meat.

Laurabeth's mouth watered. If not for saving money, she'd have accepted the kind supper invitation.

Turning to retrieve her basket from the aisle seat, she detected the same pungent odor she'd smelled many times when visiting the Galveston wharves.

Whiskey.

Leaning against the back of her bench was the stranger. "Is this seat beside you taken, my pretty lady?"

She faced forward, frozen by the rasp and slur of his voice.

A tall, middle-aged woman entered the car and clomped toward them. Bright red hair charged out from underneath a nest-like hat with velvet robins perched around the brim. She carried an enormous carpetbag decorated with the same, stuffed birds.

The stranger placed a hand on Laurabeth's shoulder and lowered his head. Hot breath crawled across the nape of her neck. She directed her eyes toward the woman, yet still couldn't move.

"I said ... my pretty temptress ... is—"

"That seat's taken." Without warning, the woman raced ahead and swung her bag in a wide circle, ramming the stranger's side with a powerful blow. He fell backward into the aisle, gasping for air.

"Keep your filthy paws to yourself."

Laurabeth quickly retrieved her basket and hat from the open side of the bench as the woman plopped down.

"Now get on outta here, you mangy scalawag, before I call the conductor."

Cursing under his breath, the man raised himself off the floor. They watched him wobble forward and exit the car.

The woman eased her bag from lap to floor, then thrust out her right hand. "I'm Cleopatra Cole. Mama give me that name when I was born 'cause I reminded her of a petite princess. Most folks call me Cleo."

Still in shock, Laurabeth hesitantly grasped the strong fingers and palm. She'd rarely shaken hands with a woman, much less one with a bird's nest on her head. "I'm ... L ... Laurabeth Appleby."

"Listen, honey. Don't ever let an old boozer get that close again, unless ..."

"Ma'am?"

"Unless you're a-courting." She roared with laughter. "You're lucky I come along."

"Thank you," was all Laurabeth could say. Then she remembered her basket. "I'm having a biscuit. Would you like one?"

"Done ate, but I appreciate the offer." Cleo scooched the carpetbag beneath her tent-sized skirt. "These days, a delicate lady can't trust the traveling public." She removed her hat.

Laurabeth bit into a flaky biscuit. She'd never met anyone like Cleopatra Cole, whose bangs puffed just above her eyebrows.

Cleo settled back into her seat. "I'm traveling north to live with my brother in Fort Worth. It's a rough town, especially for those who ain't used to residing so close to the frontier. Don't suppose that's where you're headed?"

Chewing rapidly, Laurabeth swallowed so she could answer. But Cloe talked on.

"I used to live in Fort Worth 'til Mama got sickly, so I moved here to Richmond. Doctored her for two years. I ain't no real doc like Daddy was—God rest his soul—although a girl could be if she made up her mind. Ever known any female physicians?

"Not that I remem—"

"Daddy boasted I inherited fine medical instincts. He's correct. Except Mama's strong as an old mule and twice as ornery. About drove me to an early grave. Where you from, honey?"

"Galvest—"

"I remember taking the stagecoach to Austin once. Swore I'd never do a fool thing like that again. You ever ridden on a stage?"

"Not since—"

"Most uncomfortable form of travel known to woman. Might as well ride a sidesaddle made of nails. And all the dingy riffraff a fine lady must encounter. Why one time ..."

Laurabeth smiled. Cleo reminded her of Sister Deborah— always asking questions, never waiting for answers. Mary Michael said Deborah loved to hear the sound of her own voice. The other nuns secretly dubbed her "Sister Rattletrap."

Passengers trickled back into the coach with no sign of the stranger. Considering how he could've boarded from the rear, Laurabeth refused to turn around. Perhaps Richmond was his destination, or he'd chosen to avoid Cleo and ride in a different car.

"All aboard!"

Lawanda and Chester slid into their bench as the train lunged forward. After a round of introductions, Cleo's endless questions began, matched only by the persistent clickety-clack of the rails.

The couple responded with a series of interrupted replies before facing forward and snuggling their heads together.

"Either of y'all ever been to New York?" Cleo didn't wait for an answer.

None was given.

Laurabeth yawned. The drone of her newest friend's babble on top of a full stomach made her eyes droop. Smokey shadows created by the flickering gas lamps gave the passengers an eerie appearance. She sank into an uneasy sleep.

An hour later, she awakened and made a trip to the necessary room. Except for Cleo's ragged snoring, the coach was quiet. Laurabeth returned to her seat when the scratch and flair of a match caused her to glance toward the rear. A suppressed squeal slid down her throat as dark eyes stared once again. Between the stranger's teeth was an unlit cigar. Instead of lighting it, he let the match burn. This time, he didn't smile.

Laurabeth tried to sleep, but as soon as she'd drift off, the stranger would light another match. When she finally slept, scenes from the horrible fire engulfed her dreams.

She and Sister Mary Michael drove the wagon into the city that day to buy bolts of cloth for the orphanage. On the return trip, they stopped at the Appleby estate so Laurabeth could retrieve a blouse she'd accidently left. She'd also remembered some smaller dresses stored in the third-floor attic, perfect for the younger girls.

Searching through a maze of past clothing, they discovered a trunk of her mother's things, including her wedding gown. Giggling to the point of insanity, they tried on every item, but lost track of time. Hot orange light filtered into the dusty attic room through a small decorative window. Thinking the glow was sunset, they hurried to collect the smaller dresses before dusk fell. Then Laurabeth caught a whiff of something burning. Thick smoke exploded into the room.

The roof was on fire.

Dropping everything except the wedding gown, they escaped down the topmost stairs. Flames shot throughout the house. Dense smoke clouded their vision. Laurabeth located her parents' second floor bedroom, grabbed her father's sea chest, and stuffed the gown inside. She stumbled down the main staircase to his study, located his pipe, then continued on to the parlor to rescue the family Bible. Sister Mary Michael trailed close behind, screaming they must get out.

Laurabeth wouldn't listen.

Leaping over a burning rug, she touched the Bible, then noticed the hem of her skirt was on fire. She stomped at the flames as smoke clogged her lungs.

Everything went black.

The next thing Laurabeth knew, she floated in the backyard cistern with Sister Mary Michael, while fire poured out of a molten sky. Her best friend had not only saved the trunk and precious Bible, but their lives a well.

As the locomotive chugged across Texas, Laurabeth drifted in and out of her vivid nightmare. The coach bumped to a sudden halt, awakening her in an icy sweat. She opened her eyes long enough to see Chester and Lawanda wave goodbye, then shuffle up the aisle. The train must've arrived at Temple.

Two hours later, Laurabeth roused after another stop. Her nose signaled a foul warning. The stranger's liquor? She peeked over the back of her seat, though no one was about. Cleo lay sprawled in unladylike fashion on the Peacock's former bench, snoring louder than a sawmill.

The train lunged forward into the endless night. Laurabeth turned onto her side, slipping into an exhausted sleep.

Brilliant sunlight streamed in through the windows and stained-glass skylights. Conversation hummed throughout the swaying car interrupted by a baby's hungry cry.

Laurabeth sat up and smoothed her hair. Outside was a mixture of rolling pastures and bush covered hills. Various types of hardwoods lined the banks of a meandering creek. The bleak night finally passed. They must be getting close to Fort Worth.

She leaned forward and giggled. Cleo was still asleep, her mouth wide open, bare feet and ankles draped across the narrow aisle.

The train slowed beside a sparse settlement of log buildings. Two barefoot boys in homespun shirts and trousers boarded.

"Hot coffee. Just-baked bread." They scampered from one end of the coach to the other. "Fresh milk."

Laurabeth couldn't resist the delightful aromas. She motioned to the closest boy when Cleo sat up and screamed. "I've been robbed. Stop the train."

The conductor appeared in a blur, colliding with the boy selling milk. Creamy liquid sloshed everywhere.

"My bag." Cleo stood, stair stepping atop her bench. "Some lowdown, crooked horse thief stole my beautiful bag."

"Madam. Please calm yourself." White droplets dotted the lenses of the conductor's wire-rimmed glasses. "Perhaps the bag's been misplaced."

"Never. I hid it under here." Cleo hoisted her skirt, revealing the ruffled knee bottoms of her pantaloons. A man whistled.

"Madam. You must lower your garment and descend from there at once."

Cleo inched down, glaring at the flustered conductor. During the night, her mound of untamed hair had pressed into a spiked pile. She looked like a giant rooster ready for a fight. "Have you ever had your bag stolen from beneath your dress?"

"My dear woman, I don't wear a—"

"What's a lady to do when she can't trust the traveling public?"

"I assure you, madam, that—"

"And I figured trains were safe. Have you ever ridden on a stage?"

Laurabeth bit her lower lip to keep from laughing when something made her sniff. The distinctive scent of a burning cigar triggered her memory, recalling the matches and whiskey she'd smelled during the night.

Of course.

After making certain her money was secure, she wheeled her vision toward the rear of the coach. The stranger had indeed disappeared.

Along with Cleo's bag.

An abrupt realization popped inside her head, tumbling into the pit of her stomach. The adventurous West was much different than the protected places to which she'd grown accustomed. Sister Mary Michael knew there were thieves, thus was insistent upon adding the hidden pocket. And some robbers desired taking more than a girl's gold and silver coins.

Men who stared with penetrating eyes.

Eyes refusing to blink.

Laurabeth swallowed hard, lowering her gaze onto the soft curves of her changing figure. Her mouth formed a nervous half-smile. For the first time, she saw herself no longer as a growing child ...

But as a young woman.

One who prayed for a much finer man in her future than this bad-blooded stranger.

CHAPTER 3

Ben Diamond stood up in his stirrups for the hundredth time that afternoon, scanning the rim of the distant horizon full circle.

Nothing.

"Good."

He spoke softly into a stiff southern breeze before easing back down into his smooth saddle. Ever since Ben and his two companions drove the raw mustang herd across the rocky, brush-littered canyons of the Canadian River valley, there had been no sign of the wild blue stallion. And now, a day later, not a single scrubby mesquite or yucca plant dotted the dry, grassy plain.

Looping his reins around the bobbing saddle horn, Ben removed his wide brimmed hat. He pushed two fingers through curly, damp hair. The hundred eighty horses making up the remuda moved at a controlled pace in the warm May sunshine.

An old cowboy called Flannel Eye led a packhorse ahead of the group. Familiar with the desolate territory, he rode *point*. Hand Jake Crow watched mid-herd in *swing* position, while Ben handled the backside or *drags*. At twenty, Jake was only a year older than Ben, but considered it juvenile to drive horses, much less bring up the dusty rear.

Ben patted his mount's sleek tan neck. Even though he'd been hired on as a lowly wrangler, he finally worked for a real cow outfit. One day, he'd advance to an official hand. As far as Ben could see in any direction lay the largest ranch in the world under one fence.

The XIT.

Developed by four Chicago businessmen, the three-million-acre spread was divided into seven divisions stretching over two hundred miles along the western edge of the Texas Panhandle. The northernmost division—Buffalo Springs—was where the remuda originated plus acted as headquarters for the entire operation. Orders were to deliver the mustangs to the southernmost division—The Yellow Houses—to help receive some sixteen thousand head of cattle.

"I saw you a-looking, boy," came a blurry voice from behind. "Searching for your mama? Bet you ain't never been weaned." Jake shook with laughter, then spit toward Ben's horse causing the young gelding to shy.

"Shut your mouth, Crow." Ben boiled inside. How dare Jake make comments about a mother Ben never knew. He wanted to dive off his mount and make the older boy eat his words, but that might cause the horses to stampede. Besides, Jake outweighed Ben by twenty pounds and was drinking.

"Still watching for that blue outlaw stallion I shot at yesterday, ain't ya? I do believe you've taken a shine to that troublemaker."

"He's no outlaw, and you know it."

Jake slipped a longnecked whiskey bottle from his saddlebags and took a healthy swig. "Tried to stampede the herd the first night out."

"Flannel Eye said it was a lobo."

"Ain't no wolf that big. If you believe a worn-out geezer wearing an eyepatch, then you really are a grade-A tenderfoot."

Forming a hard fist, Ben tried to control his temper. Jake couldn't see reason while sporting liquor. Drinking was against XIT rules, though it didn't seem to matter on the trail. Even Flannel Eye enjoyed a few nips around the campfire.

"Ever heard of a murdering mustang named Diablo?" Jake edged forward.

Ben chose not to answer.

"Means devil. I figure Diablo sired that miserable bag-o-bones. Reckon you could say he's the blue's pa. Worst outlaw horse to ever roam the Texas plains. Trampled five men before he died."

"Being his offspring don't mean nothing."

"Don't it?" Jake urged his mount to within inches of the gelding. "Ever hear of *bad blood*?" He leaned in close. "Runs rampant in some families. Next time I see that worthless plug, I'll fire a bullet through the middle of his cold heart. They'll call me a hero. You'll still be trying to suckle your mama."

Rage pulsed through Ben's veins. If clobbering Jake meant a stampede then so be it. Ben swung a wild fist but met only air. The older boy anticipated the reaction and toed Ben's horse in the flank, making him buck. The next thing Ben knew he was swallowing Buffalo grass. Jake howled with laughter before disappearing around the far side of the herd.

Embarrassed, Ben remounted. A burning sensation seared his conscience. Was Jake Crow aware of Ben's past? His real folks?

Six months after Ben's birth, he was taken in by Jon and Vehlma Ericksohn, a strict, God-fearing Swedish couple who ran a dairy near Dodge City, Kansas. The Ericksohns already had two school age girls and a baby boy. Even though Ben had blue eyes, he often wondered about his brown hair and lanky build when the rest of the family was stocky and blond.

On the Sunday of his twelfth birthday, Ben made a decision to follow Christ and was baptized into a local church. After the service, three parishioners congratulated Ben, but the majority left without a word. During the wagon ride home, the Ericksohn family was unusually silent. "Lucky for you the good Lord saves those who ain't deserving," Jon said, but that was the only comment anyone made.

Later that afternoon, while the others weren't around, Vehlma asked Ben to fetch a pail of water. When he returned, she admitted he was adopted, telling him the truth about his past.

Ben's natural father, a former cowboy named Ray Diamond, went bad. He'd worked for a trail outfit driving Longhorn cattle up from Mexico before deciding on a more lucrative endeavor—bank robbing and lawmen killing.

While Ben was still a baby, Ray was caught and hung by Texas Rangers.

Rose Diamond, Ben's mother, worked in a Dodge City saloon. Folks swore she and Ray were never legally married because a bartender performed the ceremony. When the story of Ray's hanging reached Dodge, Rose became wary of her role and headed north. She left infant Ben with a girlfriend, who turned him over to the Ericksohn's church. Rose was never heard from again.

For the first time, Ben understood why most folks treated him unfairly. To earn spending money, he'd applied for odd jobs on numerous occasions, yet was turned away. At social functions, people pointed and whispered, their condescending smiles angering him most. The rudeness even happened at church.

Judging him by his pa's behavior was flat out wrong.

Clearly, the Ericksohns didn't care for Ben as they did their own. Upon the rare instances they showed compassion, son Lester grew instantly jealous, provoking Ben into a fight. Sometimes, Vehlma listened to reason. However, Jon was quick to take Lester's side.

As the years passed, Ben was treated more and more like a hired hand. He disliked the dairy. Worse was his disdain for the Sunday hypocrites, so he only attended worship when forced to go.

Ben even stopped talking to God.

His greatest joy was watching the countless, bawling beef herds rumble past on their way to market. When dust clouds hugged the horizon announcing the arrival of new cattle, Ben stopped his monotonous milking long enough to sneak to the top of a small bluff. There, he'd wait for the men in high-heeled boots and colorful bandanas to race by on their spirited ponies.

When a cowboy waved his hat or shouted a greeting, Ben stayed longer, his heart pounding for the freedom of the open range. He knew his tardiness meant the stripes of a leather strap seared across his buttocks. Yet the stings only deepened his desire to join the herds, to one day operate his own ranch. Ben's plan was to save every penny.

When the time was right, he'd begin the journey to lose his pa's shadow, cleansing the Diamond name.

The Christmas Ben was sixteen, Jon unexpectedly gifted each boy his own horse. Ben's mount wasn't as expensive an animal as Lester's but was still a sleek, buckskin gelding. That evening, when Ben went out to milk, he discovered Lester severely beating the young gelding with his dad's leather strap. In a wild rage, Ben tore away the weapon, jerking it tight around Lester's throat. By the time Jon came to the rescue, Lester was purple. Jon grabbed a coiled rawhide rope and flailed Ben until his shirt was shreds of dripping red. Jon then banished the Diamond *bad blood* off his place forever. After letting Vehlma secretly doctor his wounds, Ben gathered his few possessions, mounted the buckskin, and rode south.

Flannel Eye's booming voice chased away Ben's thoughts. "Let's make camp, boys. Up ahead is Palo Duro Creek. If we're lucky, there'll still be water.

Sure enough, there were shallow pools. The remuda drank eagerly.

The old cowboy dismounted and dumped the little sheepherder's tent off the packhorse. He glanced at the mid-afternoon sun, then slid out one of the tent poles and laid it on the ground, pointing the sharp end south. "In case the morning's cloudy and there ain't no sun," he mumbled.

Ben grinned. The sky wouldn't be overcast unless the drought broke. However, like the ocean, the grass-covered plains looked the same in every direction. This part of Texas was a sea of buffalo grass. With no landmarks, the tent pole was an ingenious way to keep heading in the right direction. He'd remember the idea for future use.

"I ain't gathering no stinking cow chips tonight," Jake announced.

"You will if you plan on hot coffee." Flannel Eye frowned. "But first we gotta hobble them horses. Don't want no lobo stampeding the herd."

The tedious process began by surrounding the remuda with a single rope stretched between their three mounts. Once the triangular makeshift corral was complete, each animal was lassoed. A small piece of hemp was then secured in figure eight fashion around the front legs, just above the fetlocks. The simple system allowed grazing with short steps yet made running impossible.

Jake cursed the backbreaking chore then grumbled to Ben about the old man's ignorance. When Ben didn't agree, Jake switched his indignation to the blue stallion, continuing threats to destroy the steed if he ever saw him again.

By sundown, the remuda was hobbled. Flannel Eye ordered the corral undone. "Now I'm gonna show you two shorthorns how to stake your saddle horse in a country where there's more women than stake pins."

The weathered hand was correct. Ben could count the number of girls he'd seen since arriving at the XIT on one finger ... and she was married.

Flannel Eye attached one end of his lariat to his horse's halter, then tied a knot in the other end. After unsheathing his spare hunting knife, he dug a fist-wide hole elbow deep. Slipping the blade through the knot, he placed the knife crosswise in the bottom and tamped in the dirt. At the end of a long rope, a horse couldn't apply enough torque to pull free.

"Stake your mounts, then grab an empty toe sack. Go in opposite directions and fill 'em with prairie coal."

Flannel Eye glared at Jake. "I don't want to hear no more complaints, neither. Sky's almost dark."

Cattle hadn't roamed this section of the ranch in months, so Ben traveled a fair distance before locating a decent supply of chips. He topped a slight rise, squatted down and began filling his sack. Instantly, he became aware of a dark blur headed straight toward him. Charging through the dusky twilight, the magnificent stallion blew in from the west with the speed and color of a mighty Panhandle thunderstorm. Before Ben could react, the blue Mustang spun only feet away before vanishing from sight.

Ben coughed up dust, stood, and wiped his eyes. His heart leapt into his head, pounding in his eardrums. "I'm gonna name you Storm," he whispered. "You could've killed me. But you're not like your pa ...

"And I'm not like mine."

CHAPTER 4

Gripping her basket in one hand, Laurabeth adjusted her straw hat and stepped off the train into the crisp morning air. An excited tremor made her insides quiver.

Fort Worth.

With luck, she'd find Uncle Eustus.

The pungent odor of cattle droppings filled her nostrils, making her nose wrinkle.

"Don't smell nothing like the Gulf coast." Cleo lumbered down from the coach and drew in a huge breath. "Ah ... the aroma of grass digested into cash. Better get used to the smell, honey. We're standing at the gateway to the west."

"But I don't see any cows."

"Over there." Cleo pointed across the crowded depot to rows of tin roofed sheds. "That there's where the stockyards begin. If you think the odor's sweet today, wait until a decent rain." She erupted into a belly laugh.

"Cleopatra?"

Laurabeth turned to see a giant of a man wearing a plaid shirt, denim britches, and scuffed leather boots. His red nose, sunburned cheeks, and white beard made him look like a western version of Father Christmas.

"Colt." Cleo attacked the man with a forceful bearhug, popping his hat off his bald head like a cork from a bottle. "This here's my baby brother, Colt Cole. Mama named him after a male foal 'cause he was birthed similar in size."

"Howdy ... ma'am." Colt's face reddened deeper as he nodded at Laurabeth, then stooped to retrieve his hat. A bone-handled pistol was holstered at his side.

"Colt's in the horse-breaking business," Cleo continued, "'cept when he's the one who gets broke. I'm the only person he trusts to doctor him back into one piece."

"How's Mama?" Colt asked softly.

"Too ornery to die. But we can discuss her later. This here young lady is Laurabeth Appleby from Galveston. We're giving her a ride over to ... now where you headed, honey?"

"Dawson's Boarding House. But you don't have to—"

"Mattie's Place," Cleo corrected. "I've never met Mattie Dawson, although folks say she's a fine woman. Ain't that right, baby brother?"

"Folks say."

"Some tell how Mattie's a real southern lady. When her husband was killed by the Yankees at Gettysburg, she moved to Fort Worth and opened a boarding house. Ain't that so?"

"Some tell."

"'Course, Daddy fought in the war and never came home either. Colt was too young to remember much about that. Weren't you too—"

"Ma'am?" Colt faced Laurabeth. "Got any luggage?"

"Just a small trunk." Laurabeth thought briefly of her own papa's stories about fighting in the War Between the States. "My things will be unloaded off the baggage car."

"Guess what," Cleo thundered. "My bag got stole. I lodged a formal complaint with our spineless conductor, who wouldn't even stop the train to demand a formal search. You just can't trust the traveling public these days. Remember when I rode the stage to Austin?"

Laurabeth suppressed a smile as the horsey woman with the bird nest on her head rattled nonstop to her timid brother, forcing him to answer questions.

What an odd pair.

After locating the sea chest, Colt helped Laurabeth into the rear seat of his one-horse buggy. Cleo hiked her skirt and climbed up front. "A proper buggy's the only way to travel. I'll ride shotgun."

The wide dirt streets of the business district were laden with horse-drawn vehicles of every size and description. Brick buildings sporting various advertisements painted on their upper stories packed in amongst smaller wooden storefronts. Women wearing sunbonnets scurried about with shopping baskets, their long skirts dragging snake-like designs in the fine dust. Barefoot children scampered by on their way to school.

Laurabeth peered from side to side and rubbed her damp hands together. Even though anxious about meeting her Uncle Eustus, she was amazed to see so many rough looking men already crowding into the countless saloons. Like Colt, they were dressed in western garb and wearing pistols. Most wore shiny spurs that clinked as they stomped across the weathered plank sidewalks.

Were these men real cowboys?

As the buggy dodged pedestrians and squeaked over wagon ruts, Cleo served as an unofficial tour guide. "That there's the telephone exchange. Boasted over forty customers their first year. And that tall building way over yonder is the M.P. Bewley flour mill. M.P.'s daddy was a steamboat captain up in Kentucky. You reckon bag snatchers ride on steamboats?"

At the corner of Commerce and Third, Cleo bolted out of her seat and stood on the running board. "There's the Greenwall Opera House. Ain't it fancy? Folks swear it cost a king's ransom."

"Folks do swear," Colt and Laurabeth replied in unison. He turned around and grinned.

Shouts echoed up ahead as a man tumbled through the swinging doors of the White Elephant Saloon. He skidded chin first into the dirt and lay motionless. An aproned bartender rushed out, dumped a bucket of water on the back of the man's head, then propped him against a hitching post. The man's face was smeared with blood.

Laurabeth winced and covered her mouth.

"Fellow just earned hisself a dishwater bath," Cleo said matter-of-factly. "Must've cheated at cards and got caught."

"Must have," Colt agreed.

"Lucky to be going home with a bloody nose instead of a bullet hole."

"Lucky to be."

The business district ended with a lumberyard, the dusty road leading across a dry creek and into a residential section. Colt reined the buggy onto a treelined street, pulling up in front of a neat, two-story whitewashed frame home with a shake roof. A covered front porch supported half-a-dozen rocking chairs, plus as many spittoons. A faded sign hung crooked above the front steps:

Welcome to Dawson's Boarding House.

"Mattie's place." Cleo removed her hat and fanned her face. "You're on your own now, honey."

Colt helped Laurabeth down from the buggy, unloaded her trunk and basket, then hauled them to the porch.

"Let us know if you need anything." Cleo stood atop the running board in stocking feet. "Colt's place is just north of town. Everybody out that way knows us."

"Thank you." Laurabeth swallowed. "Thank you for—"

"Don't need to mention any gratitude, honey. I was glad to have some decent conversation for a change. Mama don't let nobody get a word in. Never has. Huh, Colt?"

"Bye, ma'am." From the driver's seat, Colt tipped his hat and grinned.

"Gonna be a scorcher today, ain't it." Cleo fanned harder.

"Gonna be." Colt urged the horse forward,

"Mama sure flaps her jaws when it's hot, complaining about every little thing. I'll swear, the next time that little woman ..." Cleo's endless blabber trailed out of earshot.

Laurabeth climbed the front steps, swallowed again, then rapped on the tall screen door. Comforting odors of lemon oil and hot soapy water wafted from within, reminding her of cleaning days as a child. She raised her hand to knock further when a pleasant voice called.

"Come on in."

A spacious entry hall opened into two large chambers before leading to the bottom of a wide staircase. The room on the right was furnished with overstuffed chairs and sofas. Bookshelves lined the far wall.

"I'm in the dining room."

Bearing left toward the voice, Laurabeth encountered a massive oval table beside a long, polished sideboard. An odd assortment of straight-backed, cane bottomed chairs were scattered about. A woman wearing a yellow apron crouched beneath the table on hands and knees, her silver-blonde hair gracefully contained in a crocheted snood.

"Looks like a pig ate here." She laughed merrily, though didn't look up. "You'd think my boarders were raised in a barn. Please carry the eggs on back to the kitchen."

"Pardon me. I'm looking for my uncle, Eustus Appleby." Laurabeth cleared her throat. "Does he still live here?"

The woman popped her head out from under the table. "Well, I'll swan. A female Appleby if I've ever seen one. Not that I have, mind you, but the resemblance is fascinating." She rushed to her feet. Thought you were the grocer's girl. I'm Mattie Dawson."

"Laurabeth Appleby."

"Uncle you say?" Mattie thought for a moment. "Then you must be Jonathan's only child."

"You've met Papa?"

"Never had the pleasure."

"So my uncle talks about him?"

"Only when tricked." She laughed, then smoothed her starched apron. "I look a mess, but tell your folks to come right in."

Pressing her palms against the sides of her skirt, Laurabeth stared at the floor. "They're ... um ... not here. Five years ago, Mama died from yellow fever. Two years later, Papa's ship sunk in a bad storm. I've come alone."

"Bless your little heart." Mattie sighed and leaned against the table. "All the way from Galveston?"

Laurabeth nodded.

"Have you been staying with relatives?"

"No ma'am. Saint Mary's Orphan Asylum." She raised her chin and made eye contact. "My Uncle Eustus is the only family I have left. So if you'd please tell me which room is his, I'll—"

"No one's here right now, dear." Mattie daubed her brow with a lacy handkerchief. "My it's hot. I do believe I've begun to glow. Let's go sit a spell out on the veranda. Will you join me for lemonade?"

"Yes, ma'am."

"Good. I've just squeezed a fresh batch. Even have bread that's been rising about ready for the oven."

Mattie ushered Laurabeth out the front door, chose two shaded rockers and soon returned with a wooden tray presenting a ceramic pitcher and matching cups.

"Thank you." The cool liquid felt heavenly to Laurabeth's dry mouth. She'd not had a drop of anything wet since the train."

"Now then, dear." Mattie took a sip. "About your uncle." She paused. "I'm afraid that—"

"Is he still alive?"

"Oh my, yes. That wonderful man has more life in him than folks half his age. However, he hasn't been around here for over a year. Moved out on the Texas frontier to a town called Colorado City. Last I heard, he was hauling freight for that big XIT Ranch up to some area they call the Yellow Houses."

A ball of despair welled up in the back of Laurabeth's throat and rolled down to the pit of her stomach. Not crying was an extreme effort.

"Now don't worry, dear." Mattie reached over and patted Laurabeth's leg. "I've considered your situation and have developed a plan. Around here, good help's in short supply. Why don't you stay and give me a hand until your uncle returns."

Laurabeth's face brightened. "He's coming back. When?"

Mattie scrunched her eyebrows and swallowed more lemonade. "Don't quite know. But the man promised he'd come back while we're both still young." She laughed.

"I've heard that before." Laurabeth frowned.

"You have doubts?" Mattie appeared slightly ruffled. "I'll admit your uncle may be long winded, plus a little crusty around the edges. But if there ever was born a gentleman of honor, it's Mister "Useless" Appleby."

"Useless?" Laurabeth didn't know whether she'd just been scolded, or to laugh at the mispronunciation.

"His nickname." Mattie chuckled. "Guess no one's called him Eustus since before his rangering days."

"My uncle was a Texas Ranger?"

"Is there any other kind? You'd better close your mouth dear, before you swallow a fly."

A slight tingle crept up Laurabeth's spine. "Why the nickname? Did he do a poor job?"

"Heavens no, gal. Your uncle was one of the most feared lawmen to ever risk his life for the sake of justice."

"I don't understand."

Mattie leaned close, as if whispering a secret. "You couldn't trade a plate of spoiled beef for the man's skill with a pistol. He was absolutely *useless*. But when it came to a rifle, he was deadly."

"So why did he stop rangering?"

"Got shot in the knee during the war. You'd never know, 'cept he limps a little during damp weather. After the knee healed, he found it pained him too much to ride a horse.

"I see."

Did Papa know his brother was a Texas Ranger?

"Now ... most men would've sat around and sulked the rest of their days. Not Useless. He's got too much spunk. The man knew exactly what he wanted so went right out and bought a wagon and a pair of mules. Been freightin' ever since."

Laurabeth scooted to the edge of the rocker and took a final sip of lemonade. At the opposite end of the veranda, her trunk and basket waited where Colt had set them. Reaching down to her skirt's hem, she felt for the hidden pocket. Over half of the twenty dollars still remained.

"Did you drop something, dear?"

"Your offer for me to stay and help is most kind, ma'am. But I've decided to go find my uncle. Is there a train to Colorado City?"

"Why ... yes. The Texas and Pacific Line runs at dawn." Mattie daubed her brow with the lacy hanky. "But out west is no place for a respectable single girl."

Laurabeth considered Mattie's warning, then replied with gentle confidence. "My uncle isn't the only person who knows what he wants."

A broad grin spread across Mattie's face. "And not the only Appleby with that stubborn spirit of adventure." She sniffed. "Oops. Gotta go check my bread."

As the screen door slammed behind Mattie, Laurabeth poured herself another cup of lemonade and held it high.

"To our stubborn spirit of adventure," she toasted, then drained the contents.

CHAPTER 5

Early the next morning, as the mighty Texas and Pacific locomotive popped and hissed in anticipation of the trip west, Laurabeth hugged her new friend goodbye.

"You're sure you have enough money." Mattie straightened Laurabeth's straw hat as if she were a small child.

"Plenty."

"I've packed your basket with fried chicken and two pieces of dewberry pie. Don't wait too long to eat the chicken."

"Yes, ma'am."

"Can you remember my friend in Colorado City?" A worried expression rumpled Mattie's face. "Perhaps I should've written down her name."

"Emma Pitts." Laurabeth grinned. "She runs the Palace Restaurant and Hotel—along with her good-fer-nothin' husband."

Mattie chuckled. "You've got a memory as detailed as your uncle's. Do give that dear man my best."

"I will," Laurabeth promised. "Thank you again for the night's lodging and all the good food."

"Pshaw, girl. That's the least I could do for an Appleby."

"All aboard!"

The daylong trip was uneventful, except for the change in scenery. Gentle hills flattened into broad pastures, interrupted by fingers of deep, jagged ravines with high rocky bluffs. Strong oaks crowded onto rich rangeland beside stone-bottomed creeks but soon intermingled with patches of scrubby mesquite. While both hardwoods competed for real estate, the smaller species eventually reigned victorious due to the more arid climate.

When the sun blazed high overhead, Laurabeth finished the chicken and munched on a piece of pie. The breeze, now edged with heat, carried the sweet-dusty odor of cured hay.

The scent of the frontier.

Rounding a long curve, she viewed the train's numerous boxcars. Since there was only one other coach besides hers—neither one full—more goods than people traveled west.

This time, no stranger stared.

She drew in a deep breath, closed her eyes, and smiled. An hour passed before the need to visit the necessary room roused her from slumber. After a quick trip, she enjoyed another bite of pie before nodding off to the rhythm of the rails.

Late in the day, Laurabeth awoke to the conductor's tired call as the train slowed for its final stop. She adjusted her hat, then peered outside as a dozen small wooden buildings slid past. All in need of paint, they were identical. A larger framed structure came into view as the coach bumped to a stop. A weathered sign read *DEPOT—COLORADO CITY, TEXAS.* Underneath *COLORADO CITY,* someone had scratched *welcome* in small letters.

Laurabeth checked the hidden pocket, grabbed her basket and hurried to exit the coach.

Colorado City.

The place where she hoped to find her Uncle Eustus.

The place where she'd rediscover happiness.

"Watch your step, ma'am." The conductor cupped a hand beneath her elbow as she stepped off the coach and onto the platform.

"Claim your luggage at the baggage car," he announced above the din.

Laurabeth moved forward, then stopped in amazement. Instead of scurrying passengers, the immediate area buzzed with a congestion of mules, wagons, and men shouting orders. Boxcar after boxcar was pried open, the workers unloading everything from bacon to barbed wire to enormous burlap sacks of coffee beans. There was even a set of finely crafted bedroom furniture and a brand-new cook stove.

Upon reaching the baggage car, claiming her small trunk was easy. Yet carrying it and her food basket through the maze of unloaded goods proved a delicate balancing act. Halfway across the railyard, she tripped over a coil of rope, sitting hard on a large bolt of cloth. The little chest flew out of her arms.

"Oh no ... my trunk."

"Don't worry." A reassuring male voice spoke above the confusion. "At least you fell on something soft and unbreakable. Your trunk, though, landed on—" He laughed. "I've still got the big toe on my other foot."

Laurabeth turned toward the voice. Papa's sea chest rested atop a shiny black western boot. Flames shot into her cheeks. "Are you all right?"

"I am now." He shoved the trunk off to one side revealing a long scuff mark, then extended her a hand. "Name's Brett

Castle. Around here, ladies allow their husbands to carry their luggage."

"Yes, but ..." She was too embarrassed to look at him. Yet, when she gripped his smooth fingers and stood, her gaze was drawn to his. "I'm not married."

"Then let me venture a guess. You're traveling with your fiancée, and he's busy buying tickets for the next train."

Laurabeth giggled. "I've come alone." She wanted to explain, but the combination of his thick dark hair and green eyes left her breathless.

Eyes the color of mid-summer leaves.

Brett's smile gleamed white and flawless. Turning his head, he yelled at an elderly man loading a nearby wagon. "Deliver this trunk to wherever this lovely young lady is staying."

The man stepped forward, removed his hat and nodded. An unsightly scar ran across a large portion of his forehead. He wore a scraggly white beard and only had one ear.

Laurabeth tried not to gasp.

"So, where might that be?" Brett spoke softly.

She swallowed. "Where I'm ... staying?"

The perfect smile returned. "Someone's family home? A hotel, perhaps?"

"Perhaps. I mean, a hotel. Yes. The Palace Hotel."

"The Palace," Brett shouted to the man, who'd already returned to his work.

Brett refocused his attention toward Laurabeth. "May I take you there in my private buggy?"

The sudden invitation made her lightheaded. She'd not considered the train depot being located on the outskirts of town. Yet both Cleo and Mattie Dawson had warned her about trusting folks she didn't know.

"Is the Palace too far to walk?"

"Depends if you want to arrive before nightfall." He offered a slight bow, then gestured to a shiny two-seater pulled by a pair of sleek matched horses. "A beautiful girl wandering about the frontier without an escort wouldn't be fitting. I'm going that way anyway."

She felt her cheeks grow warm. No man besides Papa had ever referred to her as *beautiful*. "You're sure the hotel's on your way?" The question allowed her an instant to study him closer. He wore no hat and dressed in pressed trousers with a starched cambric shirt.

"Across the street from the Palace is my family's business, Castle Mercantile, the largest handler of dry goods and hardware in this part of the state."

"Then, sir, thank you for your kind offer."

After helping her into the buggy, Brett leaped eagerly into the opposite side and scooped up the reins. He sat closer than she anticipated, but probably needed the extra room to control such a frisky team.

"You." Brett called to the one-eared man. "Move those goods out of my way."

The heavy cloth was haphazardly stacked atop the platform, causing the topmost layer to spill. Laurabeth felt sorry for the bent little man, whose beard dripped with sweat. However, he seemed used to the backbreaking work, performing each task without complaint.

When the way was clear, Brett shouted a final command. "If you want your money, old timer, you'll go straight to the Palace, then across to the wagon yard. I'm not paying for detours."

Without looking up, the man raised his hand in compliance.

Laurabeth silently questioned Brett's rudeness. Or was he simply being responsible. His family did own the mercantile.

A sharp tinge of doubt invaded her consciousness. Could she have misjudged this handsome stranger? Papa had operated his own shipping business for years. As far as she knew, he'd never spoken to an employee in such a demeaning tone.

Brett continued. "I want that load of merchandise on the road up to the Yellow Houses by first light. Scratch that expensive cookstove and you won't see a penny." He popped the reins, and the team sped away from the platform.

"Yellow Houses?" *Hadn't Mattie mentioned that same name?*

"Newest division headquarters on the southern range." Brett raised his chin. "Castle Mercantile is the main forwarding and receiving agent for the bottom half of the XIT ranch."

"The XIT?" Her suspicious tinge surged into an excited tingle.

"Since Colorado City is the nearest railhead, most goods purchased for that end of the ranch are ordered through our company. Last year, the XIT bosses hired so many freighters, we were forced to build our own wagon yard."

Pure joy pulsed within Laurabeth's soul. "Then you know them?"

"The bosses?"

"Freighters." She felt as if she'd just uncovered buried treasure.

"To know a stinking freighter is to smell one." Brett formed a haughty grin. "They're the scum of civilized society."

"I don't believe you."

"No?" He raised his eyebrows. "Take old One-Eared Charlie back at the depot. Owes his worthless life to me, and what thanks do I get."

"No one's life is worthless." Laurabeth didn't intend to openly disagree, but a sudden passion for family loyalty made her brave.

Brett frowned, then continued. "Saw his abandoned wagon and found him close by, half dead. He'd just been paid and was supposed to be working."

"Perhaps the incident wasn't his fault."

"Wrong. Made one of his famous *detours* to the back country. Got drunk on rotgut."

"Rotgut?"

"Homemade whiskey. When he was good and loose, somebody stole his coins, then dumped him in a dry creek bed. For fun, they cut his forehead and sliced off an ear."

Laurabeth gasped.

"A real shame about the ear." Brett's mouth formed a satisfied smirk. "The ancient fellow was already deaf as a post."

Instead of offering a response, she faced forward.

"You don't' appreciate playful humor?"

"Not when the joke isn't funny."

"Then, as your escort, please allow me another attempt."

She offered a slight nod, wishing she'd never accepted the buggy ride.

"As you say, all freighters *aren't* worthless."

"Thank you."

"They're just naturally stupid." Brett roared with laughter.

When they reached town, the team slowed. A dusky twilight faded into night amidst the glow of kerosene lanterns inside various shops and private dwellings.

Laurabeth rubbed her palms against her skirt, hoping to soon reach the Palace. The distinctive edge in Brett's bold laugh frightened her, much coarser than the gentle cackle he'd produced when her trunk landed on his foot. She shivered, glad she'd not mentioned Uncle Eustus.

While turning a corner, Brett slid even closer, tugging the team to a crawl. "You're a lucky woman to have bumped into an educated man way out here. One who spent an entire term at a college back east."

"That's nice." She was afraid not to respond.

"And then my father developed a bad heart." Brett cocked his head toward Laurabeth, speaking in low tones. "So, I sacrificed my law degree to return and save the family business. One day the mercantile will be all mine. Even now, I own a half interest, inherited two months ago when I turned twenty."

She glanced in his direction. "That's, um, nice as well." The overpowering scent of his hair tonic made her queasy.

"So ..." He squared his shoulders. "How about an intimate supper with a wealthy business owner?"

"You've already been much too kind." She slowly turned her gaze forward, searching for the Palace Hotel.

Tightness gripped his voice. "Then show me your appreciation by accepting my offer. You must be famished."

"Oh, but I'm not, b-because I've already eaten." She gestured toward her food basket. "Fried chicken and apple pie. I do appreciate your kind invitation, but the long train trip has left me exhausted. I'm sure you understand."

Instead of issuing a rebuttal, Brett scowled, then whipped the team into a fast trot.

Laurabeth released a silent sigh. Near the end of the street, a two-story frame building emerged out of the approaching darkness. *Palace Hotel & Restaurant* was painted white across the upper section in bold letters.

With a loud grunt, Brett wheeled the buggy into a dimly lit alley, then jerked back on the reins. The team skidded to a halt.

"Is this a rear entrance?" Laurabeth's voice trembled. "I think—"

"Think?" He laughed. "Not until you're properly educated." His voice was gravel. "First, you must learn how girls out here return a man's kindness."

Gathering her skirt and basket, Laurabeth attempted to exit the buggy, but Brett grabbed her arm. "Let go of me! I'm not hungry."

"I am. Famished for a kiss. Beautiful girls worthy of my time desire to kiss me. Why are you so selfish?"

For an instant, she stared at him in disbelief. How could a complete stranger demand she share an act so personal? Something she'd been saving for a special beau.

And then she understood. His green eyes held that same lustful gleam as the stranger's.

Brett forced a coarse laugh. "Perhaps you've never been with a real man." He dragged her close, twisting her arm.

"Stop. That hurts."

"I'll show you exactly what hurts."

"Help! Someone help m—"

He smacked a hand over Laurabeth's mouth, knocking her hat onto the seat. Gripping the back of her head with his free hand, Brett uncovered her mouth and smashed his lips against hers, forcing her down upon the seat.

Tears of fear and anger stung her eyes, followed by a sudden dizziness. How could she have let this horrible event happen? How could she have been so naïve. The odor of his sweat mixed with hair tonic made her want to vomit.

Out of desperation, she groped for something to fend off her attacker.

Help me, Lord. Please!

Grasping a single rein, she yanked with all her strength.

The spirited team lunged left forcing Brett to release his hold. Grabbing her hat, Laurabeth slid off the seat and caught her dress on an upholstery tack, tearing the hem. The money from her hidden pocket spilled onto the floorboard. Bolting from the buggy, she ran toward the Palace Hotel without looking back.

CHAPTER 6

The Palace Restaurant and Hotel was much too plain to feed and house any implied royalty. However, when Laurabeth rushed through the squeaky front door, she felt as though she'd managed to fight her way out of a snake-infested moat.

To her disappointment, the lobby was vacant of guests, and no clerk waited behind the registration desk.

What if Brett followed? Grabbed me again.

Turning an ear toward the main entry, she listened for footsteps. Her arms trembled.

Could anyone hear me scream?

Would they care?

A panicked wave of fresh tears reddened her eyes. She wanted to run, needed to hide, but her legs were lead. And then her gaze fell upon the torn hem of her best dress. She remembered a dreadful ripping noise, followed by the faint clink of coins landing upon the buggy's floorboard.

How dare Brett steal her papa's final gift.

Instant anger steadied her nerves and dried her tears. Brett had forced a kiss, though she'd *not* responded in kind. The kiss she'd saved for a special beau remained untarnished. Relief lightened her legs. And then she recalled a sound more disturbing than the dropped coins.

The rhythm of Brett's laugh—calculated and sinister.

At least he'd stolen only her money.

Light streamed into the rear of a long hallway as an inside door was thrust open.

Someone must be coming.

Yet only muffled voices and the delicious aromas of hot food wafted into the lobby. Laurabeth's stomach growled. She'd forgotten about the restaurant.

"Need a room?" A thin, stooped woman wearing a greasy apron appeared behind the desk.

"Oh ... I didn't realize anyone was here."

"S'pose your family will join you directly." The woman flipped open a worn guest ledger. "How many folks will there be?"

"You don't understand. I've traveled here alone looking for—"

"So it's a meal you're after?"

"Pardon me?"

"No money I suspect." The woman slammed the ledger closed. "Should've guessed the minute I seen you."

"But—"

"There's a tub full of pots and pans that need scrubbing. Got strong fingernails?"

Laurabeth peered down at the flap of material that once held her money.

"Answer me, gal. I ain't always this generous." She leaned forward and studied Laurabeth's hands. "You're lucky to have caught me away from the kitchen during supper. 'Course if my good-fer-nothing husband didn't wile away his days card playing, he could watch the front desk. But that would be as big a miracle as a soaking rain."

"Are you Emma Pitts?" Laurabeth remembered Mattie's silly impression of her friend.

"I am." Emma straightened and folded her arms. "Do I know you?"

"Oh, no, ma'am. This kind lady I know, Mattie Dawson, said that—"

"You a friend of Mattie's?" A weak smile spread across Emma's lips. "How in the world is she?"

"Very well."

"Tried to get her to move out here years ago, but Mattie's too refined to live on the frontier."

"Yes, ma'am."

Emma's smile melted into a hard expression. "Alone, huh? Did Mattie send you here 'cause you got into ... trouble?"

"Trouble?"

"Be honest now, gal. How far along might you be?"

"Far along?"

"This ain't no time for playing games." Emma eyed Laurabeth's middle. "You're a skinny one all right, but I reckon you'll show soon enough. Mattie knows that a gal in trouble can't hide her growing child forever."

"No," Laurabeth blurted, realizing the kind of *trouble* Emma inferred. "Mattie didn't send me here for that or any other reason. I've come from Galveston in search of my uncle, Mr. Eustus Appleby."

"Ain't never heard of no Eustus Appleby." Emma raised her eyebrows.

Laurabeth felt as though she'd been slapped in the face. Then she remembered. "Around here folks probably call him Useless."

"Why didn't you say so?" Emma laughed crustily. "That old freighter sure has a surprise waiting when he rolls down off the XIT."

"When do you expect him?"

Emma shrugged. "Tomorrow. Next week. Next month."

"Might anyone at Castle Mercantile know?" Laurabeth cringed.

"Doubt it. Useless works for hisself most of the time. Might've contracted other freight jobs around the ranch. Besides, there's thieves and rattlesnakes on that Yellow House road. Plus a rumor's been flying 'bout a band of Comanches hiding out in the Colorado River breaks. He's gotta go through there. For all I know, your uncle could be dead."

Laurabeth's mouth quivered. She refused to cry in front of this outspoken woman. "Then I'll have to go find him."

"Listen gal ..." Emma place both hands on her hips. "Ain't no stage that runs between here and the XIT. Besides, that ranch is no place for the likes of you. Why, I don't know if there's another female on the entire spread."

A shout for more grub echoed from the far end of the hallway. Emma ignored the plea. "If you know what's good for ya, you'll stay here and wait. If you ain't got no money, reckon I might let you earn your keep 'til Useless gets back."

"That's a very kind offer, but—"

"Wonder how long a soft city gal might last?" Emma stroked her chin, then strode out from behind the desk in a wide circle, as if considering the purchase of livestock. "Since you're a friend of Mattie's, I'll give you a chance."

"Thank you ... however—"

"Is that yours?" Emma pointed a bony finger toward a small alcove beside the entryway.

"Oh ... Yes, ma'am." Laurabeth had been too upset to notice her papa's sea chest.

"Take it to the last room at the top of the stairs, street side. Tonight's stay is on the house. You'll have to start work in the morning or pay cash. I'll expect you in the kitchen by 4:00 a.m.

Laurabeth nodded.

Another shout echoed from the restaurant.

"I've got to get back before they start eating the furniture. If you want supper, don't wait too long to claim yourself a plate." Emma started down the hallway, then did an about face. "You ain't never said your name."

"Laurabeth Appleby."

"Uh-huh. If you got any sense, Laurabeth, you'll get to bed early. You look done in." Emma turned and headed back toward the kitchen.

A refreshing breeze filled the upstairs room, furnished with a lantern, bed, and washstand. Emma's shocking news about Useless perhaps being dead pushed Laurabeth toward tears once again, dissolving her appetite. Not eating would prove regrettable, especially since she'd left her food basket in Brett's buggy. Though for the moment, she didn't care.

Peering out the open window, she hoped the cool night would clear her mind. There were no gas street lamps, but the moon was bright. Across the street, the enormous brick structure housing Castle Mercantile loomed in the shadows above the wagon yard. One-Eared Charlie's rig sat loaded and ready to roll.

Thank goodness Brett's nowhere in sight.

The flicker of an orange flame from the wagon yard startled her, though it was merely the beginnings of a campfire. Five men soon gathered, their voices inaudible and sprinkled with laughter. One man swigged from a jug, then passed it to the next freighter.

Are all of them lowlifes?

And then she recalled Emma's haunting warning about possible dangers.

Thieves.

Rattlesnakes.

Comanches.

Laurabeth shivered.

If her uncle was ... dead, the journey from Galveston became a foolish waste. Hot tears puddled beneath her swollen eyelids. Even if she found him, what if his trouble with Papa was irreparable?

What if Uncle Eustus refused to even speak to her?

And if that weren't enough, a handsome man in a fancy buggy stole her money after trying to take advantage.

The shiver returned, chilling her spine. She'd not realized until now, but Brett hadn't displayed the decency to ask her name. The only sensible solution was to earn train fare back to Galveston as quickly as possible.

"Oh, dear God, help me." Her whisper resonated into a sigh.

If only Sister Mary Michael were here, she'd know what to do.

At once, distant memories flooded Laurabeth's thoughts. On a similar moonlit night, they'd dared each other to scale to the top of the girl's dormitory. At over three stories high, the roof was off limits and dangerously pitched, but that's what made the trek fun. While Laurabeth hung on for dear life, Mary Michael climbed higher, finally perching atop a bell tower. Flapping both arms, the nun squawked like a crazed seagull until a sudden wind gust pushed both girls into a desperate panic. That's when Sister Mary Michael quoted a verse from the book of Isaiah.

"But they that wait upon the Lord shall renew their strength;
they shall mount up with wings as eagles;
they shall run, and not be weary;
and they shall walk, and not faint."

The sight of a frightened sister quoting holy Scripture in the middle of the night, while perched atop the lofty bell tower of a girl's dormitory made Laurabeth giggle. Mary Michael shot back a wide grin. Both girls laughed out loud, the act enabling them to gather their wits and scoot down to safety. Laurabeth had never forgotten the words that calmed her fears.

Shifting focus to the wagon yard, she watched as the circle of freighters continued to enjoy nips from the jug. Their wagons remained lost in the shadows, except for One-Eared Charlie's, the rig blanched in white moonlight. A thick tarp covered the contents.

"Oh my." Laurabeth popped a cautious hand over her mouth. Why hadn't the thought occurred sooner. All she'd have to do is wait.

Just past midnight, the last freighter wrapped up inside his bedroll, stretching out beside the campfire's glowing embers. Soon, his snores joined in the chorus of others.

Laurabeth stepped away from the open window.

I think I'm ready.

After mending the torn hem of her travel dress, she'd slipped on fresh underclothes. Not wishing to draw attention by hauling water, she'd elected not to wash her hands and face. Her final chore was repacking the little sea chest. The Bible, pipe, and wedding gown had survived the journey thus far without incident.

Donning her straw hat, she encircled the chest with an arm, then tiptoed downstairs and out the front door. Laurabeth paused to listen. Snores still buzzed from the circle of freighters. The moon, now smaller, had risen high into the frontier night, One-Eared Charlie's wagon now partially engulfed by shadows. Standing on the tongue, she loosened the tarp enough to wedge her trunk underneath.

Then slipping in beside it, she lay atop bolts of cloth, catching the whiff of a grainy aroma.

Raw coffee beans, the same comforting smell as in the hold of Papa's ship.

Laurabeth snuggled beside a soft bolt. The XIT couldn't be far, half a day at most. Her plan was to remain hidden—and safe—until the wagon arrived. She'd learned her lesson about accepting offers from a man she didn't know.

Exhausted, she fell asleep.

CHAPTER 7

Brett Castle downed a mouthful of whiskey, then pulled a gold pocket watch from his vest and frowned. The evening hadn't progressed as planned—the time now midnight. If he didn't draw a decent poker hand soon, he'd be forced to write IOU's to the Dry Bone Saloon. The girl's money helped but would soon disappear. Finding her dropped coins was sweet, especially after the way she'd teased him. Yet no dollar amount could quench the fire that continued to rage inside his mind. She was striking—more beautiful than any woman he'd ever met. Because of *her*, he'd lost the ability to think clearly.

The solution?

Marriage.

"Late for a date, lover boy?" Vernon Abbot's enormous vest-covered belly shook with laughter. The other five backroom gamblers echoed the same jovial sentiments.

"Shuffle the cards and deal." Brett glared across the table at the obese lawyer who not only owned the Dry Bone Saloon, but half of Colorado City.

Abbott cut the deck, then casually lit a long cigar. "I do believe something's affected your game, Mister Castle.

Too much strong drink, or is there interesting news you've neglected to share?"

"My private life's none of your business."

"And *my* lust for winning should never be interpreted as personal concern." Laughter echoed around the table. "However, sir, the pot's light. I cannot deal until you make your ante."

Brett slowly slid a silver dollar into the pile. His last.

"And now, gentlemen, something easy for the simple minded. A little five card stud." Abbot flicked cards around the table. "And by the by, nothing's wild except that little filly I saw 'bout sundown in Mister Castle's buggy. She seems to have muddled his confidence." Abbot chuckled. "Perhaps he should drop out of tonight's session."

"Shut your fat mouth." Brett pounded the table with both fists, sloshing whiskey and upsetting stacks of coins. "I'm not controlled by any woman."

"Merely a *simple* observation." Abbot puffed on his cigar. "I also observe you're short of funds. Didn't Daddy give you an allowance this week?"

Brett sprang to his feet. Yet before he could retaliate, two men guarding the room's entrance rushed over and pushed him down into his chair.

"Half of Castle Mercantile belongs to me," Brett yelled. "And I'll own that girl. We'll be married within a month."

Chuckles traveled around the table.

"Then if the young lady has no ill effects on your mental capabilities, I wager we play this hand blind ... if you have the guts." The hefty lawyer dealt the final card, then dug inside his vest pocket and pulled out a wad of bills. "To save time, I'll open for one thousand dollars." He tossed the wad into the center of the table.

Everyone folded but Brett, whose voice simmered with anger. "You know I don't have that kind of cash."

"Then write an IOU for something you own." Abbots lips parted into a slow grin. "How about that new buggy and matched team?"

"They're," Brett cleared his throat. "not mine."

"A shame." Abbott wagged his head. "I guess all you own that's not Daddy's is that fancy pocket watch and the clothes on your back. Of course, you could bet your half interest in the mercantile."

"You're insane."

The big man laughed so hard the floor vibrated. "Listen to him, boys. He's afraid of what the little woman might say. And they're only engaged."

"She can't tell me what to do." Brett rapidly penned the IOU and slammed it onto the pile. He drained his glass and called. "Three jacks." Perhaps his luck had changed.

"Four deuces, gentlemen. Looks like I win." Vernon Abbot jerked up the signed note. A satisfied smirk split his round face. "And by the by, Mister Castle, I may call on the little filly myself. No woman desires to share her delicacies with a poor man."

"I'll kill you, Abbot!" Brett tried to lunge across the table, but his face was immediately slammed down onto the hard wooden surface and held in place. Warm blood pooled around his mouth and chin."

"Let's not be obtuse, Mister Castle." The lawyer took a slow draw on his cigar. "I'm a fair and patient man, though I do have limits. One more violent outburst and my men will break more than your nose."

The guard released his hold. Brett slid back into his chair as a bartender hurried in to wipe the table. He handed Brett a damp cloth.

"Now then." Abbot parked his cigar in a silver ashtray. "Only a callous egotist would refuse to see how much this young lady means to you. Since I have no desire to stand in the way of love, I'll provide you with an opportunity to earn back your losses.

The sobering pain made Brett nauseous yet was nothing compared to the desperation he felt from losing his stake in the mercantile. He'd do anything to retain ownership. "I'm listening."

"Good." Abbot laced his fingers together. "You boast that in thirty days the girl will be your bride. If within that same timeframe you can come up with my thousand dollars, I'll tear up the IOU."

"Why?"

"Let's just say it's my little wedding gift to the happy couple."

"A gift?" Brett leaned forward. "What's in it for you?"

"For me?" Abbot chuckled, then unlaced his fingers. "Depends upon my risk factor. Not even something as innocent as a buggy ride with a beautiful woman is without an occasional pitfall. Therefore, I must determine if the risk's worth the investment."

Brett felt every muscle tense, though he managed to control his temper. How much did this slick lawyer know? What had he—or someone else—witnessed? "Go on."

"In language even you can understand, the deal is this. If you're *unable* to raise the grand in a month, I'll keep the IOU for your half of the mercantile. That's part one. Fair play, wouldn't you agree?"

"Depends upon part two."

"In due time." Abbot relit his cigar. "Part two means you'll also hand over your father's half of the mercantile upon his death."

Brett gulped. He was trapped. The only possible way out was to agree to terms, his chances slim at best. Acquiring one thousand dollars in thirty days was a miracle.

Abbot retrieved a folded piece of parchment from his inside vest pocket. "I've taken the liberty to draft a document concerning our business arrangement."

"Why you sorry, no good—"

"Careful there, son. Name calling will only get you into greater pain and debt." He smiled. "Just sign at the bottom. The boys here will witness."

One of the guards placed a pen and open ink bottle next to his boss.

Brett's voice shook. "You had this planned all along."

"A good businessman is prepared for every opportunity." Abbot dipped the pen, then handed it across the table to Brett. "Don't despair. Whatever the outcome, you've still got the girl. Will vows be exchanged in a church?"

Brett mouthed curses as he signed his name. No wonder he was invited to gamble with this elite group. Vernon Abbott desired to own the entire town, so he waited to pounce when Brett's mind was occupied. The whole unfortunate incident was the girl's fault. Hadn't she mentioned coming to Colorado City because of the XIT Ranch?

The XIT.

"You'll have your money by sundown tomorrow." Brett flipped back the pen, a trail of ink droplets dotting the table. "Meet me at the McCormick line shack east of town."

Everyone but Abbott hooted in disbelief. "And how, sir, might you accomplish the impossible?"

"You're not the only businessman prepared for every opportunity." Brett flashed a wry grin, slugged down a final drink and swaggered out the door. The solution to his problem was so simple, he wanted to laugh. However, he'd wait 'til he reached his buggy.

While driving home, he reviewed his brilliant scheme. Unbeknownst to One-Eared Charlie, the Yellow Houses' monthly payroll was hidden in his wagon. In fact, the freighter had unwittingly carried the funds before. There was always the chance the old fool's pockets could be picked, yet the odds of thieves taking interest in a load of dry goods was remote. Brett would wait until the wagon was several hours from town, then steal the XIT payroll without disclosing his true identity.

He grinned, reveling in his own wisdom, then scratched his head. He'd need one other person, someone shady to take the fall ... just in case.

Someone he could bribe.

El Cuchillo.

The lowlife was a drifting scavenger whose name meant the Knife. As of late, he'd been slinking around Colorado City. Best of all, his services were rumored to be cheap.

Brett chuckled, his glee expanding into a long and hearty laugh. After settling his debt, he'd find this girl who was now the object of his desire. If she were smart, she'd agree to marriage so he could save face.

One way or another, she'd pay for the trouble she'd caused.

CHAPTER 8

Two and a half days after his dusk encounter with the blue stallion, Ben Diamond watched the remuda rumble into a large corral at the Yellow House Division Headquarters. A broad grin swept across his suntanned face. They'd arrived without any major mishaps.

Nearby hands who'd already stopped work in anticipation of the noon meal erupted into a chorus of whoops and whistles. Flannel Eye ordered Ben to close the wide swinging gate as the men hastened over to inspect their new mounts.

Jake Crow wasted no time in joining the throng. "Like 'em boys?" He slid out of his saddle. "I brung 'em all the way from Buffalo Springs."

"That there big paint's gonna be mine," one cowboy shouted. "Got the legs of a natural born roper."

Another man answered, "You can have the splattered plug. Got my eye on the dun. Best night horse I ever saw was a dun."

A third replied, "That's 'cause duns are so ugly they're too ashamed to work during daylight hours. Now that little bay yonder ought to make a first-rate cutter." The comments continued as other cowboys arrived and hooked dusty boot heels over the bottom fence rail.

Ushering his mount away from the commotion, Ben cocked his hat. The sun blazed directly overhead in sea of deep blue. After untying a bandana from around his neck, he mopped his brow. Would the dry prairie ever see rain again?

A mouthwatering smell redirected Ben's thoughts. The headquarters' chuckwagon was parked a good two hundred yards away on the other side of the corral. Beyond—a mile to the east—lay a series of sand-colored bluffs resembling little houses.

Yellow House Canyon.

The spot responsible for the division's name.

"Ain't no better eatin' than sourdough biscuits." Flannel Eye positioned his horse next to Ben's. "Unless you're also chewing on thick beefsteaks fried in a Dutch oven."

The aroma increased, making Ben's stomach growl.

"Guess I'll go hunt up the boss man before dinner." Flannel Eye gathered his reins. "You got the making of a real hand, son." Glancing toward Jake, the cowboy clicked his horse forward. "Don't know what's worse ... moaning or bragging."

Ben beamed as he rode to a nearby windmill and dismounted. While his horse drank, he surveyed the area that was now his home. The land appeared pancake flat, though upon closer inspection consisted of slight uphill grades descending into low places.

In the center of the spread sat a new ranch house with a shiny tin roof. On the wide front porch, he could barely make out Flannel Eye visiting with foreman George Landers. A large barn stood amid three small outbuildings. Nearby, the long bunkhouse was still under construction.

After splashing his face with cool water, Ben sat on the edge of the stock tank. As far back as he could remember, he'd wanted to work cattle. Here, hundreds of the bawling animals filled branding pens, while thousands more grazed in surrounding pastures. The Yellow House operation was a fine sight to behold. Perhaps one day he'd own a ranch as grand.

A loud clanging, along with shouts of "chuck" roused Ben from his thoughts. In a single mad dash, the corral fence emptied.

"Any of you mule brains who kick sand in my sourdoughs won't live long enough to beg mercy." A burly man wearing the dirtiest apron Ben ever saw stood between the cowboys and a row of Dutch ovens. Tiny balls of dried biscuit dough were caked to the dark hair sprouting atop his massive forearms. "I've a good mind to feed this grub to the buzzards. At least they got the manners to be patient."

"But, Cookie, we ain't had a morsel since before sunup," came a reply. "Your biscuits are so light and fluffy, we feared they'd float away if we didn't hurry."

"That's right," added another. "Only your tender steaks keep our belly buttons from rubbing against our backbones."

A chorus of agreements followed.

The cook erupted into a hearty laugh. "Ain't y'all a pitiful bunch of liars. If I was your pa, I'd have put you out of your misery long ago."

"If we was that unlucky, we'd've let you." Snickers filtered throughout the group.

Before Cookie responded, the foreman appeared with Flannel Eye and a smartly dressed woman.

"Ma'am." A flurry of replies coincided with removed hats.

"Men," Foreman Landers addressed the group. "This here's my wife, Betsy. Arrived today. As many of you know, she's been staying up at Tascosa until the ranch house was built."

"Ma'am," ricocheted more responses, this time with nods.

Mrs. Landers smiled. "Please put your hats back on. Manners are fine inside the house, but it's way too bright out here not to cover your heads."

The men obeyed like silent soldiers.

Betsy faced her husband. "You didn't tell me they were so obedient. However, I fear they only speak one word. Perhaps some fresh baked pies will loosen their tongues."

An enthusiastic cheer broke the silence.

"Much better." She laughed. "But you'll have to wait until my new cookstove arrives from Colorado City."

A sigh of disappointment encompassed the group.

Landers produced a folded sheet of paper from his shirt pocket. "I've received this letter from General Manager A.G. Boyce at XIT headquarters." The foreman cleared his throat. "Mr. Boyce reminds all of us about the extremely dry conditions. Even though the nights are still cool, till we get rain, fires are limited to branding and cooking."

Cookie shot a retaliatory grin. The hands remained expressionless.

"Also ... the horses that arrived today from Buffalo Springs must be broken before we can receive any more cattle."

The cowboys nodded.

"As y'all already know, most mounts will train easily enough. Yet there's always a bunch of wild ones that have a different opinion."

The nods continued.

"Since we need every piece of horseflesh, headquarters has hired a bronc buster to tame the renegades. He'll arrive within the week."

Grunts of appreciation answered.

"Now, a final matter of significant interest." He grinned. "The monthly payroll should arrive within the week. Let's eat."

Shouts of joy burst from the cowhands. Ben didn't know if their glee was about the money or the food. Probably both.

He filled his plate and sat on the ground cross-legged with the rest of the boys. Clinks of metal forks on tin plates accompanied wild tales of bronco busters and unruly horses. Ben had heard of men who made such a dangerous living, though he had never met any.

After dinner, the cowboys shuffled back to the corral and branding pens. Flannel Eye and the foreman roped out the first group of horses to be broken. Ben and Jake herded the majority of the remuda to open pasture, working opposite sides. Jake was lazy and out of sorts, his behavior nothing unusual.

At mid-afternoon, Jake disappeared. Ben didn't care. The remuda was settling into their new surroundings. Occasionally, he'd redirect an inquisitive yearling, but the animals remained content with the selected grazing spot.

As shadows lengthened toward evening, Jake returned, smelling of whiskey. "Ain't nobody on this ranch who recognizes a man's true talent." He produced a bottle. "Cut my teeth on a branding iron, yet the boss makes me babysit a bunch of worthless nags and a mama's boy."

Choosing not to respond, Ben faced forward. The horses were calm. He wasn't about to be bullied into doing something stupid.

Jake continued to grumble. "I'll show 'em my worth." After taking a final swig, he dropped the empty bottle and drew his rifle. "Gonna go shoot me some bad blood." Kicking his mount, he loped off through the fading light.

Ben ached inside. Ever since sighting the blue stallion at the buffalo wallow, he'd continually swept his vision across the blowing grasses and come up empty. Yet he knew Storm was out there ... somewhere ... still stalking the herd.

Hopefully, the older boy was too drunk to shoot straight.

And then, as if his thoughts could conjure up reality, the steed appeared, standing no more than fifty yards to the east. Ben stared in awe before watching the majestic stallion vanish into the twilight.

"I'll befriend you, Storm." Ben's vow carried atop the breeze. "Then together, we'll become a team, erasing the bad blood from both of our lives."

CHAPTER 9

A huge jolt, followed by the creak of wagon wheels awakened Laurabeth from a dreamless sleep. Every muscle in her body ached.

Where am I?

Oh yes. Hidden inside a freight wagon headed for the XIT. Laurabeth smiled, confident she'd find her Uncle Eustus until a pang of doubt nibbled her conviction.

What if I stowed away on the wrong wagon?

Raising up on an elbow, she peered out from beneath the thick canvas tarpaulin into bright daylight. The surrounding terrain was rocky and unlevel.

The Colorado River breaks.

Relieved, she glanced forward. One-Eared Charlie held the reins.

Easing back into her snug nest, she tried to stretch her legs but banged a knee against something hard. "Ouch," she mouthed. The object causing her pain was the cookstove she'd seen at the depot. Since cowboys prepared meals over a campfire, a woman might be living at the Yellow Houses after all. Laurabeth's luck was improving by the minute.

Her stomach gurgled, a reminder she'd not eaten since the train. Sister Mary Michael stated how experiencing mild hunger was good because it made one more thankful for their daily bread. "I miss my wise friend," Laurabeth whispered. "If she knew my present situation, she'd offer additional advice or keel over laughing."

As the sun climbed higher, the temperature underneath the tarp increased. At first, a soothing warmth replaced the dawn chill. However, the stuffy air soon grew hot, making breathing difficult. Trickles of perspiration dampened Laurabeth's dress and stung her eyes. Thirst burned her lips, her tongue feeling as if it were encased in cotton. Careful not to reveal her position, she arranged a small opening for the entrance of outside air. The vent worked, though searing pain knotted her left leg in a debilitating cramp.

Does this man believe in stopping?

Another hour passed before the wagon bumped to a halt above a gurgling creek. Clumps of large boulders crowded atop the steep banks, surrounded by dry brush and pungent cedar. Laurabeth eagerly listened as One-Eared Charlie poured grain into a bucket, then unhitched his team. Peeking carefully, she watched him stuff what appeared to be jerky into his shirt pocket. Grabbing the bucket, he led his horses down a winding path toward a pool of shallow water.

"Dinner," she mumbled. "Perhaps they're slow eaters."

Without wasting a second, she scrambled from the wagon and slipped out of sight behind a mesquite thicket. If she hurried, she'd have plenty of time before the freighter returned.

After working her way upstream, Laurabeth carefully descended to the water's edge, enjoying a long, cool drink. So much for rattlesnakes and other dangers. Her scheme was working perfectly.

Using caution not to splash, she scrubbed her hands and face. How lovely washing her hair would be, yet she dared not.

Without warning, a wild cry burst into the stillness.

Comanches!

I should've listened to Emma.

Terrified, Laurabeth bolted up the bank and crouched behind the nearest boulder. A shirtless warrior wearing feathers and red war paint swooped out from the brush on horseback and headed for the wagon. He waved a large knife at One-Eared Charlie, who'd just run up from the creek. The old freighter managed to dodge the attacker and reach his rifle. Before he fired, another warrior appeared.

Petrified, Laurabeth watched the second Comanche pull out a pistol and shoot One-Eared Charlie in the back. He slumped to the ground.

She tried to scream.

No breath.

Wanted to run.

Where?

A calloused hand clamped over her mouth from behind, dragging her into dense brush. Knowing her life was over, she tried to struggle as a sinking heaviness gripped her senses, making everything spin.

Arms, slow.

Legs, limp.

The instant before Laurabeth lost consciousness, she glimpsed her captor. The man holding his hand over her mouth was no Comanche.

He was her father!

CHAPTER 10

A wave of cool water sloshed against Laurabeth's face. Then another.

She pushed her palms against wet sand.

"Papa. Oh, Papa."

She struggled to sit up.

"You've come home."

Her ears roared hollow. Laurabeth tried to open her eyes.

More water, this time engulfing her hair. Now streaming down her neck and shoulders.

"I've been so lonely without you. The nuns said you were ..." The words stuck in her throat. She fought back a sob. " ... lost in a hurricane. I knew the story was false."

A gentle hand supported her head.

Her voice quivered. "Never leave me again, sweet Papa. Just hold me. Let me rest in the surf."

The water stopped, though the echo in her ears continued.

Laurabeth blinked, able to focus upon the form above her. A few more wrinkles than she remembered encircled his kind brown eyes. Hair and beard were also longer than before, though three years had passed since she'd last seen him.

His lips moved, but she couldn't make out the words. He kept stroking her forehead with a soggy bandana. Why? Had she contracted the deadly fever?

"I can't hear you, Papa. The waves are making such noise. Please speak up."

"Girl, what be your name?"

"You know my name," Laurabeth heard herself yell. Why would Papa ask such a ridiculous question unless she'd contracted the fever. If so, her shouts were only whispers. Isn't that how the doctors said Mother communicated in her final hours. How unfair to see Papa again ... and be dying.

"Child, where are you from?"

The sound in her ears diminished, her mind suddenly clearer.

Silly Papa.

She wasn't sick. The questions were part of a childhood game. A way for others to glean important information in case she were ever lost.

Why not play along.

"My name is Laurabeth. I live in Galveston, Texas. My mother is Nancy Elizabeth. My papa is the sea captain, Jonathan Appleby."

"Well, I'll be plum jiggered." The fingers holding Laurabeth's head trembled. "Ain't possible." Moisture glistened around his eyes. "J ... Jonathan you say? Sea captain from Galveston?"

Laurabeth smiled. Papa was pretending to be a stranger, an important part of the game he'd not forgotten.

"Whatever made you come way out—" He swallowed. "Little gal, I ... um ... ain't your pa."

Laurabeth blinked, unsure if she'd heard him correctly.

He continued. "But I must be your kin. Your uncle, I reckon. I'm Eustus Appleby ... your pa's *twin* brother."

The unexpected news jerked Laurabeth into a state of emotional confusion. Tears clouded her vision. Her papa had briefly returned yet was now gone. Replaced by his—

"Twin?" she whispered.

He nodded.

"But I thought you were … " Laurabeth sat upright. She wasn't sitting in the ocean surf but beside a rocky creek somewhere between Colorado City and the XIT Ranch.

Her tears increased. "Oh, Uncle. I'm so happy to see you."

The dismayed freighter scooped up a hat full of water dowsing his own head. "I'm sorry to hear about your pa." Useless removed his hat. "What about your ma?"

"Yellow fever."

He cleared his throat. "You've passed out is all." Useless pulled a stick of dried beef from his pocket. "Gnaw on this here jerky 'til the fog clears. I've got a friend to bury."

The harsh reality of the situation rushed into Laurabeth's memory.

The attack.

Rolling over she tried to stand.

Her knees buckled.

"Now you just stay put, Missy."

"Those two men killed—" She swallowed. "Were they Comanches?"

"Naw, outlaws disguised as such. Just wish I'd toted my rifle. Real Comanches would've nabbed Charlie's team." Useless jammed on his hat, stood and scanned the immediate area. "Ain't no telling where them horses scampered off to. Them and the wagon was all he had."

"Did you recognize both men?"

"One of them killers calls hisself El Cuchillo. Means the Knife. I'd recognize his blade anywhere."

79

"And the other?"

"Don't rightly know, 'cept his nose was broke." Useless rubbed his beard. "I've a sneaking suspicion there was more than a foolhardy girl hidden in that load of dry goods."

Foolhardy.

The comment pulsed energy back into Laurabeth. Uncle Eustus had saved her life yet had no idea why she'd stowed away. "So ... how did you know about me?"

"Got my mules napping in some shade a ways down the creek. Heard Charlie's rig arrive so headed in that direction on foot." Useless peered toward the wagon. "Watched you climb out."

Laurabeth frowned. "I had to get to the XIT."

"XIT?" He faced her. "A decision that 'bout got you killed."

"I was looking for you," she blurted, "the only family I have left."

Useless opened his mouth to reply but remained silent. With a pained expression, he backed in the direction of his team, then turned and disappeared into the brush.

Laurabeth stared in disbelief. Was her uncle declaring he wanted nothing to do with her?

"He hates me," she voiced to the flowing stream, "because something terrible happened between him and Papa."

Before too many tears rolled down her cheeks, self-pity evolved into anger. She wanted to fling the jerky to the minnows, then remembered the foolishness of turning down food on the frontier.

"Well ... I don't need ... Mr. Useless Appleby," she muttered between chews. "He'll never replace Papa. I'll just get my trunk and—"

A queasiness gripped Laurabeth's middle. Returning to Galveston was impossible with no money. Perhaps she could still work at the Palace Hotel, though she had no desire to be in the same town with a man like Brett Castle.

She raised her chin. "Then I'll walk to the Yellow Houses. The woman there will surely give me a job."

When Laurabeth arrived at the wagon, Useless had retrieved his rifle and was erecting a crude, mesquite cross over a rocky grave.

"I didn't figure you'd stay put."

Unsure of how to respond, Laurabeth remained silent.

"Charlie never wanted to be buried in no dark box." Useless glanced at her through sad eyes. "Just can't figure what he hauled that was worth killing over."

She climbed into the wagon. The so-called Comanches had cut away the tarpaulin, but the little sea chest wasn't where she'd placed it. Maybe its location had shifted during travel. After a frustrating search, she found the chest near the front of the load.

"What's that?" Useless stood on the wagon tongue, an unlit corncob pipe clamped between his teeth.

"Something my papa gave me." Laurabeth knew her answer sounded crisp. She tried lifting the trunk without success.

"Let me help you."

"I can manage."

Before she protested further, Useless stooped over and raised the chest, balancing it atop the narrow sideboard. "You packing bricks in there?"

"Personal items." Laurabeth leaped out of the wagon. This time, her curt reply bordered upon disrespect. But why be polite to a man who wanted nothing to do with his own blood relation.

"My personal items ain't that heavy."

"No?" She smoothed her dress. "Kindly hand over my belongings, and you'll be rid of me."

Useless chuckled. "Did you sit on a cocklebur, Missy? Why so riled?"

"Just give me my trunk, and I'll be on my way."

"Figuring on walking back to Colorado City?"

"Absolutely not. I'm going on to the XIT. There's a woman there who might—?"

"Alone?" The pipe fell from his teeth.

"I don't need your permission."

He grimaced. "XIT's at least three days from here by wagon. And that ranch ain't no place for a single gal who—"

The trunk slipped off the sideboard and crashed against a sharp rock, spilling stacks of twenty-dollar gold pieces."

"Well I'll be plum jiggered. Them are some right weighty personal items."

"Where are my things?" Laurabeth dropped to her knees in a frantic search. "Mother's wedding gown. Our family Bible."

"You sure that fancy box is yours?"

"I'm certain." Leaning closer she noticed the latch. "There's no initials."

Useless squatted down, then retrieved a piece of paper amidst the coins. "This here's the monthly payroll for the Yellow House Division." He slapped his leg. "That's what them rascals were after."

Once again, Laurabeth couldn't contain her tears. "Papa's trunk held all that's dear to me. Now everything's gone." She tried to stand, but her legs wobbled. "I was foolish to come."

"Whoa there, Missy." Useless helped her stand. When she was steady, he grabbed a bolt of cloth from the wagon, making a seat in some thin shade.

"Thank you." Laurabeth sat.

"What you need is a hearty meal and cup of strong coffee, 'cept there ain't time. When those two scoundrels realize they've plucked the wrong goods, they'll hightail back here faster than a scalded jackrabbit."

She heard his warning, though didn't care. After risking her life to save the precious belongings from the fire, the items had become her little family. And now, two men she'd never met had snatched them away. She clenched her fists.

Useless continued. "Somebody local knew about the hidden payroll. Means our best bet is to transfer Charlie's load to my wagon and haul the goods on up to the Yellow Houses. Traveling empty in that direction looks suspicious." He studied the horizon. "If we head back to Colorado City, we're liable to get ambushed before we get there."

Laurabeth glanced at the man who dared look so much like Papa. Her jaw tightened.

"I'll plant false tracks leading back toward town." Useless waved his pipe. "Then we'll take a short detour through the brush country and head northwest, hitting the XIT road just below the caprock."

"When do we start?" Laurabeth glared at her uncle.

"Folks say El Cuchillo's getting old and drinks too much. If we're lucky, he'll miss our real trail."

"If we're not ... and he finds us?"

A grave expression spread across the freighter's weathered face.

"Please tell me." Laurabeth stood. "I've come this far and deserve to know."

"I ain't worried about El Cuchillo." Useless faced her. "His partner's the coldblooded killer."

A familiar tingle of determination gave Laurabeth new energy. She refused to let anyone destroy her vow of finding lasting happiness.

Especially a coldblooded killer.

CHAPTER 11

In ten minutes, the sun would finish its lazy descent behind the western horizon. Brett Castle faced forward, then glanced over at the wooden chest strapped behind El Cuchillo's saddle. Inside was over a thousand dollars.

Brett smiled.

His father usually attended to the Yellow House payroll that arrived under guard each month from XIT headquarters in Chicago. However, he'd felt poorly so asked his son to doublecheck the amount, then pack the coins into their smallest, ordinary, shipping trunk.

What a stroke of luck.

After slowing his horse, Brett motioned for El Cuchillo to do the same. They were less than a mile from the McCormick line shack.

The ride had been quiet. Upon removing the feathers and war paint, they'd taken their time, even swallowing a little cheap whiskey along the way. Vernon Abbott and his fellow henchmen would already be there. The thought of making them wait until the last possible moment made Brett giddy. The sum he owed was a pittance to the greedy lawyer's overall worth yet would foil his plans of acquiring the mercantile in thirty days. Therefore, any amount of nervous anticipation was slow torture. How satisfying to see the fat man sweat.

Brett chuckled. The robbery was easy. He'd never shot a man in cold blood, so killing One-Eared Charlie proved bothersome at first. Though after a few sips of whiskey, Brett convinced himself the murder was an act of mercy. Odds were good the deaf old fool would step on a rattler and die a painful death. Besides, there was one less freighter scumming up the frontier.

"You should not have killed that man." El Cuchillo hadn't spoken since the attack. "You should have let me handle him."

"And do what?" Brett scoffed. "Threaten to add his other ear to your collection? He wasn't drunk this time and would've filled you with lead."

El Cuchillo frowned. "Learn patience, *mi amigo*. You will live longer."

Ahead, a lone rider slipped from the shadows into view. As the pair rode closer, an additional set of hooves stamped at the rear. Brett pulled gently on his reins. The rider blocking their path was the same man who'd broken Brett's nose.

A gruff voice threatened from behind. "Don't try nothing. I'm watching your hands."

"Nice to see you ladies again." Brett twisted around slowly and tipped his hat. "May I have this dance?"

"Shut up," ordered the man in front. "You've kept the boss waiting. He's not pleased."

The sound of a pistol cocked from behind.

Without further discussion, Brett and El Cuchillo were ushered to the empty line shack. Red-faced, Vernon Abbott puffed a short cigar while sitting astride an enormous white gelding. The midnight gamblers—also on horseback—completed the group.

"You're late." Abbott flicked a cone-shaped ash. Great rings of sweat circled out from both armpits, soaking the sides of his linen vest. He glanced at El Cuchillo. "Does the little missus approve of the wholesome company you keep, Mr. Castle?"

Tense laughter volleyed about the group.

"I brought the money." Brett focused on Abbott. "Hand over the contract."

The lawyer took a final drag on his stogie, thumping it into the dirt amidst a scatter of sparks. "You surprise me, Mr. Castle. One thousand dollars is a staggering amount for a poor man. I think you're bluffing."

Brett formed a slow grin. He'd beat the power-hungry ogre at his own game.

Abbott ordered the chest unbound from behind El Cuchillo's saddle. With a scowl, the lawyer balanced the chest against his stomach. "Seems light." He released the brass latch.

"Feel free to grab an extra couple of dollars." Brett smirked. "Consider the coins as your modest tip."

The lid popped open. A startled smile trailed between the big man's ears. "Why, Mr. Castle ... I believe you've handed me your personal belongings by mistake." Abbott held up a pair of lacy underdrawers. "Do all the men in your family wear these?"

The group exploded with laughter.

"Give me that chest," Brett yelled.

"And look here, boys. He even brought along his own wedding dress, plus a Bible for the preacher."

Brett leaped off his horse, as did Abbott's men. In an instant, Brett's arms were twisted behind his back, a heavy fist thrust into his gut. One of the gamblers pointed a pistol at El Cuchillo.

"Not yet." Vernon Abbott's words were barely audible. He dropped the trunk, nudging his mount within two feet of where Brett was doubled over. "Do you consider me a fool?"

"An ... honest ... mistake." Brett fought for air. "I'll ... get ... your money."

Abbott's face was purple. "My time *is* money, Mr. Castle. Moreover, I've grown weary of your childish games. Yesterday, my guards broke only your nose. Today, you won't be as lucky."

"Ooh." Another inch and Brett knew his right arm would crack. "Two thousand. I'll pay two thousand dollars."

The gamblers heehawed.

Abbott ordered silence. "As I earlier stated, I'm a fair and patient man, though not stupid. If you can't raise the thousand, how do I believe you'd double that amount?"

"There's a way."

"A grand will still suffice." The lawyer's lips parted into a devilish grin. "Remember our pleasant chat about my risk factor?"

Brett groaned.

"I'll take that as a yes. Due to your comical charade this evening, you've now only ten days to raise the cash."

"You can't do that. I signed a contract."

"Oh, didn't I tell you?" Abbott dug inside his vest with two fingers. "That particular document was misplaced. So I've drawn up another for your convenience."

"Why you sorry—aww." Brett dropped to his knees, the excruciating pain making him retch.

"I said not yet." The lawyer drew a long-barreled pistol, pointing it inches from Brett's temple. "A man unable to pen his name would be better off dead. Don't you agree, Mr. Castle?"

"I'll ... sign."

"Excellent. The boys here will witness."

Cursing his rotten luck, Brett stood as the gamblers galloped away under a full moon. Had some traitor at the mercantile switched the payroll with a trunk of women's things?

Not likely.

Or did One-Eared Charlie have a lady friend?

Impossible.

Brett rubbed his aching arm. At least, it wasn't broken.

"Have some whiskey." Having already drained one bottle, El Cuchillo uncorked another. "The amber spirits will numb your pain."

Squatting down, Brett easily lifted the wooden chest. "Get out of my sight, you drunken fool. Anyone with a brain would know the weight of a thousand dollars in gold."

"I will do as you ask, but know this. He who plays poker with Vernon Abbott is the idiot."

The brass latch gleamed in the moonlight. Something caught Brett's attention.

El Cuchillo downed another swig, then pointed his mount in the direction of Colorado City. "I will see you soon, *mi amigo*, to collect the many coins you've promised."

Brett wasn't listening. Furrows creased his forehead as he studied the latch. "The initials J.A.," he whispered, "I've seen them before."

Peering at his dusty boot, he ran a finger along the scuff mark.

Of course. The girl's trunk.

He remembered how she'd babbled about the XIT, wanting to go there.

A broad smile spread across his face.

She must've stowed away in One-Eared Charlie's wagon.

And then, a sudden realization pounded his memory.

His smile vanished.

She probably witnessed the murder.

He shivered.

Could she have recognized him?

Impossible.

Though because One-Eared Charlie was old and half blind, he and El Cuchillo were sloppy with their disguises. She was young and could see clearly.

Brett paced, cursing his sour turn of luck. He couldn't chance discovery, having seen men guilty of lesser crimes swing from the end of a rope. The sight wasn't pretty.

A chilling sweat moistened Brett's brow, his breathing now rapid. And then a flicker of an idea nudged his frenzied mind. Since One-Eared Charlie was dead, the beautiful girl was lost on the lonely freight road.

Frightened.

Hungry.

Pausing to examine the thought, Brett offered a throaty chuckle. His best bet was to rescue her. Take her the little chest, saying how it was picked up outside of town by one of the Company's freighters. Explain how he'd remembered her, determined what happened, thus rushed to her aid.

He'd be her hero, vanquishing any future pairings with One-Eared Charlie's murder. Not only would Brett get the money—still located inside the old man's wagon—the girl would gratefully accept his love and marry him.

A rogue remembrance spanked his ego.

His muscles tightened.

What if she refused his proposal? That meant he'd have to finish what he started in the buggy, *making* her love him.

A harder slap.

What if the scheme to win her affection failed?

Brett clinched his fists as anger pulsed through his veins. How dare she spurn his love? Due to her selfishness, he'd be forced to play one final hand. Then as with One-Eared Charlie, Brett would also leave *her* for the buzzards.

After all … Comanches were rumored in the breaks.

CHAPTER 12

A gentle predawn glow lit the fringes of the starry eastern sky. Laurabeth yawned as she stretched her aching limbs. There wasn't a muscle attached to bone that didn't complain. Following the attack, her uncle planted false tracks back toward Colorado City, then discretely reined his team onto an abandoned military supply road. For the remainder of the day, the journey was a constant jolt. Odds of being followed by the so-called Comanches made the detour necessary, though at times the path amounted to little more than a washed-out buffalo trail.

Bunching a heavy blanket around her shoulders, Laurabeth peered outside her uncle's freight wagon. She heard the whir and spatter of grain poured into a wooden box, followed by soft crunching. Uncle Eustus was feeding his team. There still wasn't enough daylight to distinguish one animal from the other. He treated the pair as family, dubbed "Mister" and "Mizz," the largest brown mules Laurabeth had ever seen.

She sighed, feeling guilty about the smug way she'd acted.

Why do my emotions fly out of control, spinning me to the wrong conclusions?

Yesterday's lengthy escape from danger proved Uncle Eustus didn't hate her after all. Even though he insisted upon calling her Missy, he'd referred to her as *his niece* when conversing with the team. Last night, he'd persuaded her to sleep on a soft bedroll inside the wagon. He'd slept atop the hard ground underneath, wrapped in only a thin rain slicker.

"We'll stock up on blankets and other supplies when we reach Old Man Singer's Store," he'd said casually, after glancing over his shoulder for the hundredth time. Yet, a deep concern occupied his eyes, the same look Papa wore when a dangerous storm brewed out in the Gulf. The possibility of more trouble made Laurabeth's skin crawl. No wonder her uncle kept his rifle by his side.

Was life this precarious in his rangering days?

A sharp pop returned her thoughts to the dawn. There was a flurry of stamping hooves, followed by a series of loud brays.

"Now, Mister, keep your thieving lips on your side of the feed box." Uncle Eustus raised his voice above the commotion. "Mizz, keep your hind feet to yourself."

Laurabeth giggled. Uncle Useless sounded like one of the stern sisters. Perhaps he should start an orphanage for homeless mules.

"You awake, Missy?"

"Yes, Uncle." Laurabeth sat up and ran a hand through her tangled hair. She'd give anything for a brush.

"Best not to attract attention with campfire smoke down here. We'll be on top of the cap soon. Once there, I'll stand at the edge, then look back across the lowland and see if anyone's following our trail." He opened a squeaky trap door on the side of the wagon and rummaged through foodstuffs.

"The cap?"

"Caprock." He chuckled. "Reckon it's as much dirt as rock since all that grass grows."

He held up a large tin can and squinted at the label.

She wondered if more cold beans were in store for breakfast, then remembered not to complain about food on the frontier. "How big is the cap?"

"Goes north for a couple hundred miles. Maybe more. Cap's what the Texas high prairie sits on. Guess that's what makes it so high." Digging a pocketknife from the front pocket of his overalls, he sprang the blade. "Soon as I stab open this here can, we'll eat."

The final star faded into deep blue as pink and orange hues announced the sunrise. There wasn't a cloud in the sky. Laurabeth stood and smoothed her wrinkled calico. She put on her hat and climbed out of the wagon.

"Ain't bacon and sourdough biscuits." Useless handed her a fork. "S'pose anything that won't bite back will do in a pinch. Hope you like tomatoes."

At this point, she didn't care if he'd served the same bitter turnip greens the nuns canned by the bushel every spring and fall. Her uncle was correct. Food was food.

Within the hour, they were rolling again and soon intersected with the XIT road. Ahead lay what looked like a solid line of flat-topped mountains.

"Is that the caprock?" Laurabeth wrestled with her hat due to a sudden breeze.

"Yesum." Useless adjusted his battered felt and grinned. "Better clamp that fancy straw down tight. This little gust ain't nothing to the constant blow up yonder on the *llano*."

She'd intended to comment on being used to the wind, even liking it, but her uncle'd spit out another strange word. "The what?"

"Llano Estacado. Means *Staked Plains*, named by that Spanish explorer, Coronado.

"I don't understand."

"They say he chose the name 'cause of the tall yucca stalks that shoot up outta the grass like—"

A roadrunner dashed out of the brush.

"Like tent stakes?" Laurabeth wrinkled her nose. Papa had great fun teasing her. Perhaps her uncle did too. "Is that true?"

"Can't rightly say 'cause I ain't no history scholar. Besides, words from back then might mean something different now. Plus, there ain't that much yucca." Useless chuckled. "The only *steaks* I'm privy to shoot up out of the grass have four legs and go moo."

As Mister and Mizz plodded ahead, the mesas became more distinct. Instead of an unbroken line, there were groups of enormous tables separated by rocky mounds and jagged ravines. For the remainder of the morning, they traveled parallel to the giant outcroppings. Then upon topping a slight rise, the road turned northwest. Another hour passed as the wagon descended gradually, halting beside a spring-fed creek. Looming straight ahead was the monstrous caprock.

"Last chance for fresh water 'til tonight." Useless dropped the reins allowing the team to drink their fill. "They ain't too thirsty yet, but both know what's coming. See that thin line yonder, hugging the side of that cliff?"

She nodded. A mile or so beyond the creek, an intimidating mesa rose hundreds of feet out of a deep canyon. Zigzagging up the steep face was what she hoped was a leftover buffalo trail.

"That there's our road." He grabbed the canteen from which they'd been sipping and stepped from the wagon.

"As long as we don't meet a freighter headed down we'll be fine."

"What if we do?" Laurabeth eyed the distant pinnacle and rubbed her palms. Heights frightened her. She'd panicked on top of the girls' dormitory.

"Then we'll flip a coin with the other driver to see who passes."

"If we lose?"

"Ain't never lost."

There's always a first time.

Useless slowly filled the canteen, then with a sober expression faced his anxious passenger. "You'd better hope Mister and Mizz can fly." He laughed heartily. "Don't fret Missy. The rig going up has the right-of-way. Road's wider than it looks."

They'd not ascended far when the road became shoestring skinny. At times, the outside wheels teetered along the stony edge and dislodged rocks the size of watermelons, sending them crashing into the bottomless gorge. Yet the strong mules pulled at a steady rhythm. Fortunately, they met no one. Laurabeth discovered that focusing upon the road ahead helped calm her fears. Then Useless began a frightening tale about climbing the cap in a blinding dust storm, almost being blown off.

Near the top, they rounded a bend, and the way became less steep. The team breathed heavy, their sleek sides heaving in and out like a blacksmith's billows.

"Atta-boy, Mister." Useless gently slapped an encouraging rein against the mule's sweaty rump. "Keep a goin', Mizz. We're almost there."

The wind increased as the wagon creaked up a six-foot mound of rippled sand.

Laurabeth gasped.

Without warning, the land opened into an endless sea of waving grasses.

The Texas High Plains.

A place of which she'd only read.

A place where earth and sky either engaged in fierce combat or played in perfect harmony.

A place caring little about those bold enough to enter.

Useless pulled back on the reins. "Ain't this country something?"

Speechless, Laurabeth slowly stood and removed her hat, inviting the soothing breeze to swirl about each hair strand, massaging her scalp. The climbing anxieties vanished, forever blown off the cap into the rocky depths.

After carefully scanning the lowland, Useless released a long breath and grinned. "Gotta barrel of water for the team." He stepped down off the wagon. "After Mister and Mizz have a drink and catch their breaths, we'll eat a bite, then be on our way. I want to reach the Tahoka Lakes before nightfall."

Mattie's warning of Useless being a talker proved true. Once atop the high prairie, the freighter uncorked his vocal chords. Words spewed everywhere. Throughout the long afternoon he blabbered on and on, smoking his corncob pipe, telling funny stories about freighting on the XIT.

The intense sunlight scorched Laurabeth's neck and hands. However, for the first time in days, she let careless laughter warm her soul. During a rare lull, she considered asking about her father, yet changed her mind, inquiring instead of her uncle's past as a Texas Ranger. This led to tales of a more serious nature involving interesting people she'd never met and wild places she'd never been.

The team's lengthening shadows signaled that the sun would soon dip behind the western horizon. "Tahoka

Lakes," Useless blurted, interrupting his own story. He pointed his pipe stem toward half-a-dozen distant shallow depressions surrounded by taller grass. "Only the biggest one still has water. Sure be glad when this drought's over."

No other freighters were about, so Useless halted the mules a couple of hundred yards from the largest lake. "Don't want to scare off the wildlife that waters here each evening."

After Mister and Mizz were fed and staked for the night, Useless built a campfire from dry mesquite stored underneath the wagon on a rawhide sling. He set a cast-iron Dutch oven beside the flames to warm, then added a lump of lard. Grinning, he unwrapped a pair of overalls to reveal a small wooden keg. A white substance had crusted around the rim and dripped down the sides. He raised the lid.

"Missy, this here's the staple of the west."

Laurabeth peered inside. In the twilight, the thick liquid was akin to frothy milk. A sweet yeasty odor made her stomach gurgle. "Sourdough?"

"Best this side of the Mississippi. Been nursing the same batch ever since I come out west. Makes my bread and biscuits light as a cloud. Even my cakes."

"Cakes?"

"Ain't a man allowed fine eats at Christmas?"

She giggled. He was becoming more and more like Papa.

Useless explained how yeast was difficult to buy on the frontier, so folks used sourdough instead, a mixture of flour and water allowed to ferment. "'Course you gotta keep replacing what's been used or the whole mess will die. Sometimes I add chunks of raw potato to keep the mixture bubbly." He studied the keg. "Gotta keep the contents warm, too, if you want fluffy biscuits. On cold nights, I slide the entire business inside my bedroll."

With his fingers, Useless mixed a mound of flour with salt and sugar, adding enough sourdough to form a ball. After lightly kneading, he broke off egg-sized pieces, placing them in a single layer inside the Dutch oven. "Pack 'em in tight or they won't rise."

Supper consisted of canned beans, canned tomatoes, and the freshly-baked sourdoughs. To Laurabeth, the hot biscuits tasted like rich, tangy rolls that didn't need butter. By the time they'd filled their stomachs, a blanket of darkness covered the lonely prairie. The moon had yet to rise, though thousands of stars shimmered in the clear night sky.

"Reckon I'm a might too tuckered to sit around the fire and yarn." Useless yawned. He'd just finished wiping out the Dutch oven while Laurabeth cleaned and put away the scant eating utensils. "How 'bout you, Missy?"

"Exhausted." She giggled softly. After the rigors her ears had experienced, she couldn't imagine her uncle having a story left to tell.

Minutes later, she lay once again atop the warm bedroll, her conscious thoughts fading toward slumber. From beneath the wagon, the freighter's pleasant voice slipped into yet another tale.

A sudden contentment made her smile. Instead of ocean breezes, prairie winds now blew about her life's circumstances. A single tear seeped from the corner of her eye. For the first time since Papa disappeared, she felt a spark of genuine happiness—the joy of being with family.

Rolling onto her back, she faced the speckled heavens. Her uncle's words were too drowsy to understand.

Thank you, Heavenly Father. Thank you for letting me find Papa's brother.

Closing her eyes, her mind drifted into scenes from their pleasant afternoon when a flicker of doubt raised her eyelids.

What will Uncle Eustus do with me after we reach the Yellow Houses?

She sighed. Being with her only relative was wonderful, though somehow wasn't enough. A tear leaked from the other eye. Why did she always allow sad thoughts to spoil the glad ones?

Life is so confusing, Lord.

At least her heart no longer ached, but a dull emptiness echoed after every beat. Her newfound joy had a hollow center.

Overhead, the brilliant bursting of a shooting star commanded the heavens. Before she could blink, the star connected with another. Two glittering bodies melted together in a blinding flash of silvery-white, then traveled over the horizon as one.

In that instant, Laurabeth knew how to fulfill her self-made promise of finding lasting happiness. She needed someone besides kinfolk to share her life with. A man whose hopes and dreams blended seamlessly with hers. A man to love.

A husband.

A million goosebumps popped.

The stars smiled.

He's out there.

Laurabeth sat upright, whispering surprised enlightenment into the night breeze.

"He's the reason I've come."

CHAPTER 13

Sitting astride his mount, Ben Diamond gazed across the darkened landscape. Due to high afternoon winds, he'd driven the skittish remuda down into a protected area of Yellow House Canyon. At sundown, the gale diminished, and a more relaxed herd trotted back up onto the golden prairie. The night horses were selected, then led to a holding corral while the remainder of the herd grazed beneath a canopy of glowing stars.

Ben smiled.

He was finally working toward the dream of owning his own spread. Some of the boys rumored the XIT was established for land value, meaning the raising of cattle was secondary. Plus, the entire shoot'n-match would one day be sold off in sections to homesteaders.

"That's why I've got to save every penny," Ben announced, as if the sleepy remuda was interested in hearing his plans. When the time came to buy, he'd be ready. As a respected landowner, he'd once and for all cleanse the Diamond name.

He was also developing specific ideas about cow work, toying with the vision of developing purebred herds suited for the arid high plains. Yesterday, the ranch foreman slapped Ben on the back, calling him a *natural born wrangler*. However, he could hardly wait to be promoted to an official hand. Cowboys made one whole dollar per day.

Sucking in a slow breath, Ben nudged his mount into a leisurely walk. He was happier than he'd ever been, even though something ached inside.

Something deep.

The ache wasn't a sharp physical pain, rather a dull longing. What frustrated Ben most was he couldn't pinpoint the reason. Since the feeling became more noticeable when work slowed, Ben vowed to remain busy.

Each morning before sunup, he'd grain the herd because green grass was in short supply. After breakfast, he and Mr. Landers roped out the horses required for that day's work. Next, the incoming night horses were fed, then the entire group driven out to pasture. As Ben circled the remuda, he'd carefully check each mount for problems such as galled spots or bruised feet. Since the horses were his responsibility, he strove to be familiar with each animal's distinctive characteristics.

During long afternoons when the wind was calm and the herd easy, he'd help Cookie fill the chip wagon with prairie coal.

"Boy, what's the matter with you?" The crusty cook's questions were routine. "Ain't you got something better to do?"

"Not at the moment."

Cookie wagged his head as a tobacco-stained grin bunched the stubble on his leathery cheeks. "You ain't proud like some," he'd say. "One in particular."

Ben knew who Cookie meant. Even though wranglers were expected to help gather fuel, Jake Crow felt the act was beneath him.

"Fine with me," Ben said aloud, his words nudging his thoughts back into the calm night. Things with the remuda ran smother when the complainer wasn't around. If Jake wasn't drinking, he was hung over, making his treatment of the horses just short of cruelty. Yet what charred Ben's bones even more was the way the older boy bragged, especially about killing *that bad-blooded outlaw steed.*

Ben leaned back in the saddle, diverting his glance toward a distant coyote's howl. Yet his thoughts fixed upon a desire to befriend the wild blue stallion.

"How?" His whisper carried atop the breeze. "How do I gentle the wind?"

Twice more, he'd seen Storm stalking the remuda at dusk, before bounding out of sight into a hidden offshoot of Yellow House Canyon.

Was he looking for food?

Most likely.

An idea punched into Ben's brain. The next time a freighter delivered a load of grain, he'd buy a sack and leave a little near the offshoot. Meanwhile, he'd borrow a few bucketfuls from the feed shed that he'd pay back.

Ben Diamond was no thief.

He considered his plan and grinned. Buying the grain was an investment, the first toward his future ranch operation. Storm would make an excellent sire.

A sleek golden mare offered a slight nicker. Something rustled in the dry grass and the mare nickered again. Ben turned toward the rustle. Storm stood no more than twenty yards away. The magnificent stallion rose tall upon his powerful hind legs, answered the mare with a throaty growl, then disappeared into the darkness.

Ben chuckled aloud, then spoke. "How stupid I am. Storm's not only searching for food, but for a mate."

At that moment, two shooting stars burst out of the heavens, then joined together as one. For the first time, Ben realized his mysterious hurt was for someone special. A girl to travel with on life's rugged journey.

She's out there.

He shivered.

The relationship he desired was much deeper than what the boys boasted about around the campfire. This woman would love only him, and he only her.

They would share each other's hopes.

Believe in each other's dreams.

What Ben Diamond needed most ...

Was a wife.

CHAPTER 14

Laurabeth stood atop the bouncing wagon seat and stretched. They'd broken camp at the Tahoka Lakes well before dawn. Now, another day had all but passed. Useless predicted they'd arrive at Old Man Singer's Store close to dark. The thought of seeing other people was exciting. More than that, the promise of a hot bath thrilled her toward unbridled giddiness.

"Better watch out there, Missy." The freighter kept his eyes on the road ahead. "Knew a feller once no bigger'n you who stood on the seat that-a-way when driving his team. Fell off and rolled down a prairie dog hole. Ain't been heard from since."

"Perhaps he prefers living underground." Laurabeth flashed an impish grin, twirling around like a ballerina.

"Don't say I ain't warned you."

She gazed out across the treeless plain. As with the ocean, the prairie contained huge swells. There were also numerous low spots Useless called "buffalo wallows." Most were powder dry, while some retained enough moisture for beautiful wildflowers to bloom. Deeper wallows still had small, stagnant pools from which the mules could drink.

"I feel like I'm dancing on the deck of a mighty clipper." Laurabeth uttered the words in singsong fashion, spinning faster and faster. The wagon jolted. She fell backward with a squeal.

Useless saved her with a single arm. "You 'bout waltzed yourself plum overboard, Missy." He laughed heartily. "Now sit tight and don't fret. We'll soon smell the tasty supper Mrs. Singer cooks right inside the store. Last I was there, she heaped my plate with crispy salt pork, buttered corn, and boiled potatoes."

"I can't wait." Laurabeth allowed hunger to push aside her embarrassment.

"Guess what she served for desert?"

"Pie?"

"Better." He faced her with a grin. "Stewed prunes. Ain't that some fancy eats."

In less than a mile, the forward stretch of prairie abruptly ended, the grass rubbing against a wall of sky.

"Yellow House Canyon," Useless stopped the team near the edge. "'Bout three hundred feet to the bottom. Maybe a mile across. Runs all the way to XIT land."

Laurabeth peered over the side, glad she'd stopped dancing.

"See that big lake down yonder?"

It was the most water she'd seen in one place since leaving the coast.

"Can't view 'em from here, but yonder over a slight rise are two wooden buildings. The one with the wide front porch is the store. Other one's the house."

The wagon clattered down a series of switchbacks leading to the bottom. Useless explained how ten years prior, G.W. Singer traveled to Yellow House Canyon from Iowa, settling at *Punta de Agua*, meaning Point of Water. His first customers were buffalo hunters and Indians.

"Old Man Singer's one of the kindest folks I ever met. Too generous for his own good and never locks a door." Useless nudged Laurabeth with the back of his hand. "But if you figure cheating the old man, don't cross the south end of his buffalo gun."

"I'll cross someplace else."

They laughed.

About a quarter mile from the store, Useless reared back his head and sniffed. "Dang the bad luck. The Singers ain't home. Must be visiting them Quaker families over in Estacado."

"How far?" Laurabeth felt her stomach rumble.

"Ten miles. If they ain't back before we head out in the morning, I'll settle up with the old man later for whatever supplies we need. He won't mind."

Upon entering the one-room store, Useless lit a lantern above a long, narrow counter. On one end were oval shaped jars containing varieties of stick candy. The opposite end supported a thick wheel of yellow cheese.

"Look Uncle, there's licorice." Laurabeth skipped along the counter's length. "And cheese." This *was* civilization.

Useless chuckled. "Too bad there ain't no hot supper waiting. Soon as I lay a fire, we'll remedy the situation." He shuffled toward a shiny black cookstove at the room's center. Nearby stood two crude wooden tables surrounded by benches.

Laurabeth had never seen such a range of items packed into one store. Lining the walls from floor to ceiling were shelves stuffed with canned goods, tobacco, cloth, and nails. In the rear, hundred-pound sacks of flour and cornmeal towered ten high. Adjacent were shorter stacks of salt and sugar. Boxes of potatoes lay scattered about, while onions and chili peppers hung from the rafters in bunches, producing a spicy odor.

"Oh, look." Near the dry goods, Laurabeth spied a pale pink dress of cotton eyelet, simple yet beautiful.

"Belonged to a cowboy." Useless wiped soot off his hands as the fire began to crackle.

"A cowboy?"

"Bought the dress as a wedding present for his bride-to-be. Spent his last dollar." Useless frowned. "She upped and married another fellow, so the cowboy traded the female finery for a month of foodstuffs."

Laurabeth brushed the back of her hand across the soft fabric. "Lovely." She glanced down at her own dingy calico. Days had passed since she'd torn the hem in Brett Castle's buggy. Since the disappearance of Papa's sea chest, all she had to wear was one set of clothes, even sleeping in them.

"Reckon any gal pretty enough to wear that fancy an outfit might need some additional supplies." Useless approached the counter, reached underneath and pulled out a hairbrush.

"You mean ... the dress is mine?"

"Ain't my size. And Mister and Mizz already got a brush."

A wad of emotion clogged the back of Laurabeth's throat. Once again, Uncle Eustus reminded her of Papa.

"One more thing." Useless brandished a small bottle of toilet water. "This here's so you'll stink real good." He chuckled, then cleared his throat. "I'd be willing to bet that somewhere around here there's some of them ... uh ... female under trappings Mrs. Singer sells to the ladies over at Estacado. Ain't really my affair, so you'll have to look."

"Oh, thank you." Laurabeth wanted to leap across the room and hug him, but he was already banging an iron skillet on top of the hot stove.

Supper consisted of bacon, fried potatoes'n onions, boiled corn, stewed prunes. Since both of them were famished, neither said much during the meal. After the dishes had been washed, dried, and put away, Useless emptied and rinsed a large washtub, then dumped in three buckets of clean lake water.

"As promised." He started to walk away, stopped, started, and stopped again. "I'll ... um ... go watch for any latecomers and tend to Mister and Mizz while you bathe. If I see so much as a jackrabbit heading your way, I'll holler." He jammed his pipe into his mouth and headed out the door.

From a large stovetop kettle, Laurabeth added boiling water to the tub until the temperature was to her liking. She quickly undressed, then stepped into the washtub, lowering herself into the soothing warmth. Layer after layer of dust and sweat disappeared as she scrubbed. After soaping her hair, she rinsed it with fresh water from another bucket ... brisk yet heavenly.

Allowing herself a moment to soak, she glanced over at the pink dress, then studied the little restaurant area.

The Singers must operate their business as a team.

She smiled.

What an amazing woman Mrs. Singer must be to live so far from town. Was this life her desire? Had she married the man of her dreams?

Laurabeth dried herself, thinking again about the two shooting stars melting into one.

"When will I'll meet ... him?" She wondered aloud.

By the time her uncle rapped on the door, she wore a new set of underclothes and the delicate frock. She'd even pinned her damp hair into a bun and splashed on a smidgeon of toilet water.

"Well, I'll be plum jiggered."

"You'd better close your mouth before a moth flies in." Giggling, she spun around on one foot. "Fits perfect."

She added enough water to the kettle to make coffee, while Useless stoked the fire and snuffed out the lantern. He was strangely silent.

"You look a lot like Ma," he said finally, as firelight flickered across his tin cup. "I mean the way she looked when I was a young'un."

"Papa always thought so." Laurabeth swallowed hard. She'd purposely not commented to Useless about her father since the attack. "He used to tell me stories about his growing up years. How he'd left home at sixteen to go to sea." Her hands moistened, making holding her cup difficult. "Papa never once mentioned you."

Useless sighed, set down his coffee and dug a tobacco pouch from his overalls pocket. "Well, Missy, I reckon I deserved the silence." He filled his pipe and lit it. "So how'd you know I existed?"

"From Papa's final letter. He'd heard you were in Ft. Worth and planned to go there himself. Then his ship went down, and ..." Her voice trembled.

"And you came looking instead."

She swallowed hard, determined to reveal her stay with the good sisters and the terrible Galveston fire. Yet this time the telling wasn't hard. She felt stronger. "Mattie Dawson says I got that 'stubborn Appleby spirit of adventure.'"

"So that's how you found me." Useless slapped his leg. "That Mattie's quite a gal and a bona fide talker too. Knows more about my past than I'd care to admit." He peered into the bowl of his pipe. "She's been itch'n for years to find out what happened between me and Jonathan. Just some things ain't nobody else's business less'n—" He sucked on his pipe, struck a match, and relit the tobacco.

Laurabeth tightened inside. She'd been bold and lost. Her uncle probably hated her now.

"Less'n they be family." He punctuated his statement with a puff of smoke.

As the fire shrank to glowing embers, Useless explained how he and his twin both left the mountains of West Virginia to follow their dreams. Unlike Jonathan, the inexpensive land had lured Useless down to Texas. Once there, he fell in with a troop of Rangers.

"Then the War Between the States come along." He shoved another log into the stove, his voice dry. "That's when Jonathan and me stopped writing each other. Wasn't much point."

"Why?"

"Our letters couldn't be delivered."

"Only when Papa's ship was at sea. But in port?" She frowned. "I don't understand. He was the captain."

Useless gazed into the fire. "Letters from a Confederate soldier weren't welcome on a Union ship ... and vice versa."

Covering her mouth with a hand, Laurabeth gasped. "You fought on opposite sides."

"I was wounded in the Battle of Galveston and couldn't ride a horse no more. The mortar shell that got me was fired from Jonathan's ship. He didn't know."

A tear crept down her cheek. So that's what Papa meant by "the bitter conflict."

"After the war, Jonathan tried to make amends, but I refused. We got into a heated argument about politics, calling each other names. Truth is, I blamed him for ending my career as a Texas Ranger."

"Did you ever tell him?"

Useless wore a blank stare. "Since I couldn't ranger, I hauled freight back and forth from Houston to Galveston. One day, I felt especially pitiful, so got all whisky'd up. Decided to find Jonathan and tell him how he'd ruined my life. The next thing I knew, I held a knife to his throat. Ain't touched no liquor since."

"But why didn't—?" Laurabeth could barely speak.

"I dropped the knife. The look in my twin's eye was what sobered me. All that hate from a nation at war with itself sloshed out and buried its claws deep within our souls. We vowed to never speak each other's name again."

Silence.

"I'm glad you told me." Laurabeth felt an unexpected calm. "I know Papa's forgiven you."

Useless slowly nodded. "Ain't nothing more important than your kin." He grinned. "Less'n it's your mules."

Hours later, Laurabeth felt a tap on her shoulder. She opened one eye. White moonlight flooded into the room.

"Better wake up, Missy. Got Mister and Mizz all hitched and ready to go." Useless gripped his rifle.

"What time is it?"

"Early. Thought we might as well travel while the air's cool."

Laurabeth sat up and rubbed her eyes. "You mean while the air's *cold*." She tugged the blanket around her shoulders. "What about breakfast?"

"At midnight?" He chuckled. "We can pry open some cans along the way."

"May we, at least, light a lantern?"

"What for? Moon's bright enough to see thirty miles. I'll load the last few supplies while you dress."

He'd no sooner shut the door, when she remembered seeing the rifle. Laurabeth scurried out onto the front porch.

"Well, Missy, you're a gal who gets ready quick. Figured you'd wear that frilly pink contraption. A blanket could get right warm around noon."

"What's the matter?" Laurabeth eyed the rifle.

"Gotta cover thirty miles to get to the Yellow Houses. Thought we'd best get started now so—"

"Without your coffee? I'm not budging until you tell me why we're in such a hurry."

Useless leaned against the wagon and tugged his beard. "Probably don't amount to nothing, but I got this feeling them so-called Comanches are back on our trail. Maybe no more than five hours behind. Didn't hit me 'til an hour ago."

"A feeling?" Laurabeth crossed her arms. She enjoyed staying where there was a wooden floor and warm stove ... especially in the middle of the night.

"Bore this here feeling a bunch in my rangering days. Ain't nothing I can rightly explain."

"How often were you correct?"

Useless answered matter-of-factly in the moonlight. "Every single time."

CHAPTER 15

A fading moon path stretched across Punta de Agua as Brett Castle spurred his exhausted mount down the dimly lit road into Yellow House Canyon. After the line shack incident with Vernon Abbott, he'd hurried back to the murder site to discover both the girl and payroll were gone. Fresh tracks indicated a heavy freight wagon pulled by mules carried her and One-Eared Charlie's load in the direction of Colorado City. When the trail became too difficult to follow, he'd again sought the services of El Cuchillo—not only to lay another disguised ambush, but for his keen tracking skills. Upon swallowing much whiskey, the drifter had agreed, this time demanding Brett's gold watch as advance payment.

Pulling back hard on the reins, Brett skidded to a stop. The darkened outlines of Singer's house and store showed a half mile ahead. He reached back and stroked the trunk he'd carried for the past forty-eight hours and smiled. "The girl will soon be all mine." His words spilled into the night. "She and her precious belongings."

Catching up, El Cuchillo eased his mount to a halt. "Talking to ghosts, mi amigo?" He tipped a half empty bottle to his lips, then continued. "Singer's wagon tracks head toward Estacado two days ago. Freighter's tracks lead west through Yellow House Canyon, five hours old."

Brett pounded his fist on the saddle horn and cursed. He and El Cuchillo had pushed hard and needed to rest their mounts. Whomever picked up the girl must realize they were being followed. Now the pair was too far ahead to catch.

He cursed again, realizing he'd have to forget about this particular payroll—however, there'd be others. Meanwhile, he'd bribe Abbott with the buggy and matched team to extend payback time. The greedy lawyer would be elated to draw up another crooked contract.

"We'll stop at the store to rest the horses." Brett nudged his mount into a trot. His biggest problem was still the girl, and what she might recall about the murder.

He needed to meet with her privately.

Give her the trunk.

Prove his love.

Not only would this chivalrous act forever cloud her memory, but their marriage would also allow him to save face amongst the midnight gamblers.

Brett stood in his stirrups, glancing back at El Cuchillo. Since catching up with the girl before she reached the XIT proved impossible, the old drifter's services were no longer needed. Moreover, his increased drinking slowed their speed.

"That lowlife doesn't deserve my gold watch." Making the statement aloud pushed another from Brett's mouth. "I'll need his horse for my bride."

Sitting back down in the saddle, he formed a plan. Once inside the store, enticing El Cuchillo into a little poker would be easy. Ply the man with enough whiskey and he'd pass out. Then Brett would take back his watch and steal the horse, leaving the drunken fool as a surprise guest for Old Man Singer.

"Drink up." Brett uncorked a new bottle, then slid it across one of Singer's tables. In the center, a kerosene lantern emitted a shadowy glow.

"You are most generous for one who's allowed a fortune in gold to slip from his hands." El Cuchillo looked up with bloodshot eyes. "For what reason do we drink?"

"A beautiful girl." Brett dealt from the deck he'd shuffled. "And the watch I'll win back before sunup."

The old man grinned with rotten teeth. "I'll drink once for the senorita, mi amigo. I'll drink many times for the holes in your pockets."

After winning four more hands, El Cuchillo struggled to keep his eyes open. In the midst of hand number five, he slumped over the table.

Brett smirked. "A drunkard *and* a simpleton." He stood and reached for the watch.

The drifter sprang to his feet, knife drawn. "We now play for death."

The men circled the table.

El Cuchillo continued. "Vernon Abbott makes contracts. The Blade is unforgiving."

"Death?" Brett spit out a coarse laugh, then reached for his pistol and cocked it. "Plan to cut off my ears first?"

"Along with your trigger finger, mi amigo. Then I will send you to the devil."

Before Brett could shoot, El Cuchillo lunged across the table, upsetting the lantern. Instead of steel penetrating flesh, the knife collided with the gun barrel. Both weapons fell to the floor. Brett tackled the old man, grabbing him around the waist as smoke and flames filled the room. When El Cuchillo reached for the gun, Brett gave a mighty push, flinging the drifter into a teetering stack of flour. The heavy sacks fell, knocking El Cuchillo unconscious, pinning him to the floor.

As orange flames reached high into the dawn, Brett Castle rode toward the XIT to collect his bride, her little sea chest tied tight behind his saddle. Not only had he retrieved his expensive pocket watch but acquired a new knife and an additional horse. Most satisfying, there was now one less witness to One-Eared Charlie's untimely demise.

Brett spurred his mount with renewed energy, determined to do whatever was needed to save his reputation.

And his neck.

CHAPTER 16

As the morning sun blazed across the sky, the trip through Yellow House Canyon grew breezy and warm. Except for a family of wild turkeys scuttling along the dusty wagon tracks, Laurabeth noticed no other travelers. Yet, Useless kept his Winchester at his side, urging the team forward at a steady clip. At noon, they stopped at a shallow pool for water and a quick bite to eat.

"Mister and Mizz smell rain." Useless scanned the road behind, then lit his pipe. "See how they're swinging their heads back toward the southeast after every drink."

"There's not a cloud in the sky." Laurabeth giggled. She'd never heard of mules predicting weather.

"Most times when they act this-a-way, the wind soon changes direction." He exhaled a thick puff of smoke and watched it swirl. "Yes'm. That breeze is sure enough trying to make up its mind. I'd bet the weather smarts of those two animals against anybody's highfaluting almanac."

Two hours later, they climbed out of the shallow canyon and back atop the flat prairie. Useless reined the team to a halt, then stood and surveyed the distance they'd covered.

"Ain't a soul in sight."

"You sound uncertain, Uncle."

"Do I?" He sat, then clicked the team into motion.

Laurabeth studied the endless vista. "Where are we?"

"XIT land. This here's what they call the south pasture, though it ain't completely fenced."

"We're on the ranch?" Her words colored the dry grass with disappointment. Instead of seeing rugged young men riding the range, all she saw was a windmill pumping water out of the lonely ground.

"We ain't to the Yellow House headquarters yet."

"I thought there'd be cows."

"You'd smell 'em if the wind wasn't at our backs." Useless chuckled. "Reckon them cattle can whiff that fancy toilet water you're wearing? Longhorns got good noses."

They stopped at the windmill's holding tank to water the team. Useless scanned the horizon again while praising the weather predicting talents of a good pair of mules.

Laurabeth washed her face in the cool, clear liquid. After brushing her hair, she glanced down at the pink dress. A familiar tingle danced along her spine.

Three miles further on, the wagon creaked over a slight rise. All at once she saw the cattle. Thousands of them. Circling the bawling herds on horseback were riders dressed in wide brim hats, twill shirts, denim trousers, and leather boots. Some had brightly colored bandanas tied around their necks.

"Oh my." Laurabeth rubbed her palms across her dress.

"Ain't they a sight?" Useless wore a broad grin. "Bet you never witnessed so many beeves in one place."

As the wagon passed, the cowboys stopped and stared, then awkwardly tipped their hats.

Laurabeth's face grew hot. If the cattle smelled her, could the cowboys?

Another mile passed. Large pens filled with more cattle, plus small groups of cowhands bordered each side of the roadway. An acrid odor rode the stiffening breeze.

"Branding calves ain't my favorite fragrance but must be done." Useless reached into his overalls pocket and handed Laurabeth a clean bandana. "Hold this against your nose. We'll be out of smelling range directly."

At that moment, a loud yelp sounded from a nearby cowhand, followed by howls of laughter.

Useless winked. "Guess that hand got to gawking at the passing scenery and branded hisself."

Laurabeth blushed.

"No bother, Missy. After the boys get over the shock of seeing such a pretty gal, they'll behave right mannerly." He tugged his beard. "At least they'd better."

When they rounded the final pen, the ranch and outbuildings came into view.

"Headquarters. See that chuckwagon yonder?"

She nodded.

"What say we make a beeline in that direction. I've got a hankering for fresh coffee."

The unpleasant branding odor was soon replaced with the smoky aroma of sizzling beef. Laurabeth's mouth watered. The last hot meal they'd eaten was at Singer's Store, which seemed like days ago.

"Wait 'till you get a mouthful of Cookie's sourdoughs." Useless urged the team into a trot. "Taste even lighter than mine. And his steaks are fork tender."

Thoughts of the tangy biscuits and tender beef made Laurabeth's stomach growl. Hopefully no one heard.

Useless reined the team to a stop, then hollered to a man stooped over a large mound of dough. "Ain't supper ready?"

Cookie didn't look up from his kneading. "Back so soon begging for food?"

"I only eat those dern rocks you bake 'cause I don't want the wind to carry me off."

"Needn't worry about that. The wind don't want a *useless* old coot like you."

"Well this old coot brings news for the boss, unless he up and died from that rawhide you call meat."

As the two men bantered, Laurabeth noticed a young cowboy unloading a small wagon of dried cow chips with a shovel. His back remained toward the group. She couldn't help but watch.

Must be the worst job on the ranch. Perhaps he's being punished and is ashamed.

Cookie's voice interrupted Laurabeth's thoughts. "Poor devil." Still focusing upon his work, he pinched off balls of dough, packing them into a Dutch oven. "Charlie and me go back a ways. I'd like to get my hands on the sidewinder who kilt him."

"I'd like to get my hands on a cup of that hot mud." Useless placed a forefinger against his lips, signaling Laurabeth to remain silent.

Cookie ignored the coffee insult, then called to the young man shoveling chips. "Ben?"

No reply.

"Ben? Quit your daydreaming, boy. Go fetch Mr. Landers. Ben!"

"Yes, sir?" He turned around and froze, dropping the shovel on his foot.

Laurabeth giggled.

Cookie jerked his attention toward the girlish sound, upsetting the Dutch oven. His mouth hung open. Half a dozen raw biscuits lay in the dirt.

"Ain't you two good-fer-nothin's seen a woman before? This here's my niece, Laurabeth Appleby."

Red-faced, Ben removed his hat. "Ma'am."

"Nice to meet you." Laurabeth didn't mean to stare, but this tall cowboy was the most handsome young man she'd ever met.

"So how 'bout a cup of that burnt sludge before it petrifies." Useless climbed out of the wagon.

Regaining his composure, Cookie replaced the ruined biscuits. "You ain't never mentioned no female kin."

"You ain't never asked."

Ben stepped forward, still clutching his hat. The corners of his mouth formed dimples connected by a crooked grin. "Ma'am."

"Son." Cookie raised his voice. "Don't just stand there repeating yourself. Help the lady down. Then go fetch Mr. Landers."

Removing his gloves, Ben set his hat aside and stepped toward the freight wagon. The tops of his ears glowed pink.

Laurabeth swallowed a gasp. She'd have to place her moist fingertips on Ben's shoulders. Yet her anxiety vanished the second his strong hands clasped about her waist.

"Thank you." Flames shot into her cheeks.

Their eyes met.

"My pleasure, ma'am." Ben backed up to retrieve his hat. "Guess I'd best ... um ... g-go get the foreman." Turning to exit, he tripped over the shovel, falling face down into the chip pile.

Useless and Cookie crowed with delight as Ben scrambled toward the ranch house.

"That Ben Diamond's one of the finest boys I ever run across." Cookie wagged his head. "Sure daydreams a lot."

"Ain't no harm in that." Useless poured himself another cup. "Did you know mules dream?"

"Ain't surprised. Reckon a mule's gonna do whatever a mule sees fit."

Laurabeth leaned against the wagon wheel. "Ben Diamond," she repeated softly. His name had the flow and rhythm of summer waves.

She smiled.

Ben's eyes reminded her of that magical blue expanse where ships disappeared over the horizon. The spot where the ocean stopped, and the sky began.

"I do hope you've brought my new cookstove." A woman dressed in a man's shirt and britches appeared astride a beautiful black gelding. Her blonde hair was tied up in a bun.

"Yes, ma'am, Miss Betsy. I mean, Mrs. Landers." Useless leapt to his feet. "I heard you was arriving from Tascosa."

"Useless Appleby." Betsy wore a playful, scolding expression. "Just because I'm grown and married doesn't give you permission to be so formal." She smiled, then directed her attention toward Laurabeth. "I wasn't aware you carried passengers."

"There's a lot he ain't told us." Cookie folded his arms and frowned.

A large man rode up to the group and dismounted. "So, this is the special cargo the boys are jabbering about." He tipped his hat. "I'm George Landers. Welcome to the XIT."

"Laurabeth Appleby."

While Useless explained how the payroll motivated murder and led to the discovery of his niece. Laurabeth discreetly scanned the area for Ben.

Why didn't he return with the foreman?

A sharp pain punched her insides. Had Ben heard her giggle when he fell into the chip pile? She'd not purposely laughed, but he looked both funny *and* innocent with that row of sweaty brown ringlets clinging to his forehead.

Is he disgusted with me now? Will he even talk to me?

Mr. Landers's deep voice interrupted Laurabeth's thoughts. "Those outlaws who murdered Charlie may be aligned with the newest rustler bunch."

"I figured as much." Cookie frowned.

Useless nodded. "Same gang of scoundrels who've been cutting XIT fences."

"That's my bet." Mr. Landers eyed the freight wagon. "Good work saving the payroll. Means I'll give the boys their wages after supper."

Supper. Of course. Ben had to eat, meaning Laurabeth would see him then. In fact, she'd see him at every meal.

"All the way from Galveston?" Betsy stood beside Laurabeth. "I'll bet you're completely done in."

"Thank you, ma'am, for asking, but I'm fine."

"Nonsense. You appear lost in another world." She placed an arm around Laurabeth's shoulders. "You'll stay up at the ranch house with me as long as you're here."

"Thank you." To Laurabeth, the invitation seemed more like an order.

Betsy laughed. "We'll have Cookie's tasty supper brought up to us. The unmannered boys tend to stare."

Laurabeth managed a weak smile.

Would she ever see Ben again?

CHAPTER 17

The darkness inside the feed shed suited Ben just fine. He'd bungled everything and wanted to hide from the world, especially the girl named Laurabeth Appleby.

He kicked an empty barrel. She had to be the most beautiful girl he'd ever seen.

To avoid facing her at supper, Ben decided to borrow some grain and feed Storm instead, hoping Cookie would save him back a plate. Though when word spread about the boys getting paid, Ben had to attend. Laurabeth was the endless topic of conversation yet wasn't present. Useless had delivered food to the ranch house for the ladies.

Plopping down into some loose hay, Ben released a long sigh. He'd still visit the little draw after dark. Everyone would be too busy jingling the coins in their pockets to worry about a lowly wrangler riding toward Yellow House Canyon with a bucket of oats. He'd rotated that week to the remuda's midnight watch, so there'd be plenty of time to keep an eye out for the blue stallion before going on duty.

Mostly, he needed time to think.

"So why am I disappointed she wasn't at supper?" He spoke aloud, his confusion unexpected. Was feeling this way over a girl he'd just met ... common?

Since he wasn't an official cowhand, chances were strong she'd not have an interest in him anyway.

Ben sighed.

Even if she'd been later inclined, he'd tripped and fallen face down into a pile of cow chips, ruining any future chances.

Cow chips.

He'd even spit small bits out of his mouth.

Standing, Ben punched a fat grain sack with all his strength. "Why didn't I pick up the stinking shovel. I know better."

And then the memory of helping her down from the wagon burst into his brain. The pleasure of placing his hands around her tiny waist, then being drawn to her delicate face. He'd caught a whiff of her sweetness, like prairie flowers in a fresh breeze. When her hair brushed across his bare fingers, he felt a softness he'd never dreamed existed. So soft, the feeling now hurt.

How could something be wonderful and painful at the same time?

A shout interrupted Ben's thoughts.

"You worthless excuse for an animal."

Sharp leather pops came from outside the feed shed, followed by panicked whinnies. Ben leapt to his feet and bolted into the dusk.

"I'll teach you to nip at me." Jake Crow swung a heavy bridle and bit, flogging the head of the same golden mare that had nickered at Storm. A lasso looped around her neck was entangled with her hooves. A saddle lay crumpled in the dirt.

"Stop! That mare ain't been broke. You'll put out her eyes." Ben charged the older boy, knocking him to the ground. Jake struggled, yet this time was no match against Ben's pent-up fury.

"Last straw, Crow." Ben pounded a flurry of fists into Jake's face before retreating. "Horse beating will get you fired."

Spitting blood, Jake wobbled to his feet. "So will stealing grain."

Ben retreated a step. How did Jake know? "I was borrowing. Gonna replace every bit."

"Don't matter. You still ain't nothing but a no-good thief." Jake wiped blood from his lips. "I know the truth."

"You don't know anything."

"Don't I?" Jake spit. "Heard something interesting last night. Put the facts together 'bout that killer mustang."

A sharp pain seared Ben's guts.

"Me and some of the boys were yarning 'bout thieving outlaws. Where they was from. One scumbag in particular."

"You're drunk."

"My belly full of whiskey will soon water the grass." Jake laughed. "You're filled with something that bleeds a much darker yellow. Ray Diamond's bad blood."

The stranglehold around Jake's neck was instantaneous. Hot anger clouded Ben's judgement.

Five suffocating seconds passed.

Then a scene flashed across his memory, recalling how in a previous fit of rage he'd almost ended his stepbrother's life.

He released his grip.

If Jake Crow died, Ben would be a murderer.

Just like his pa.

CHAPTER 18

For the first time in weeks, Laurabeth wore a nightgown, an extra belonging to Betsy Landers.

"The water will be boiling soon." Betsy, still dressed in riding attire, adjusted the damper on her shiny new cook stove, then spooned dried tea leaves into a china pot. "Guess I inherited my taste for the Queen's special blend from my grandmother. Did I mention she was born and raised in England?"

Laurabeth nodded, though could recall little of their one-sided conversation, her thoughts still focused upon Ben. She'd so hoped he'd have been the hand to deliver their supper.

"Cookie's coffee is a bit strong for my liking." Betsy lowered her voice. "When he's not looking, I add hot water to my cup."

"I do the same with my uncle's." Laurabeth tried to redirect her thoughts. "But I add water to the whole pot. He hasn't a clue."

They laughed.

"First time I ever saw Useless Appleby was with a coffee cup in his hand. He and a troupe of Texas Rangers were camped outside our fort. The spot was a favored site."

"You have a fort?"

Betsy filled the teapot. "Fort Mason down on the Llano River. Belonged to the US Calvary. Daddy was Colonel, and I was seven.

While the tea steeped, Betsy examined a bolt of lilac silk taffeta, telling of her fascination with the rough lawmen who seemed to defy danger. "They'd ride in for supplies and stay a week."

As Laurabeth listened, images of Ben flashed through her mind.

He's tall, yet how tall ... exactly?

"Useless was one of the few Rangers who'd pay attention to a child." Betsy handed Laurabeth a steaming cup. "He'd buy me licorice, set me on his lap and tell stories."

I wish I could sit on Ben's lap.

Laurabeth gasped, as heat rose to her cheeks, embarrassed for entertaining such a brazen idea.

"Is your tea too hot?"

"Oh. No. Thank you. All's fine." She took a quick sip.

"So ... what do you think?" Betsy placed a swath of matching velvet against the silk.

"Ma'am?"

"For the collar and cuffs of my summer dress. One never knows when dignitaries from the Chicago office may arrive for a visit." She paused. "Please call me Betsy."

"Everything's lovely, Betsy." Laurabeth pictured Ben falling into the chip pile and smiled.

"Wait until you see this fabric." Betsy untied a smaller bolt. "Striped silk for the bodice and skirt."

Laurabeth giggled.

"I guess a woman in men's trousers clamoring about a silk dress does appear a bit silly." Betsy chuckled. "I was never one for a side saddle."

"Oh, no. I wasn't making fun. I was, um ... just—"

"Nothing to worry about. More tea?"

As Betsy rattled on about dress making, Laurabeth yawned. She sipped the sweet brew while replaying the scene of Ben helping her down from the wagon. Picturing his eyes made her feel warm and cozy. Having gazed into them so intently was unlike her, plus would've been considered bold back home. But this place was not Galveston. One-Eared Charlie's murder proved that. Women on the frontier must be brave to survive.

Do bold and brave share the same meaning?

A giant grandfather clock bonged ten p.m. Laurabeth jerked with a start.

"I do believe my constant chatter has lulled you to sleep." Betsy merrily snipped frayed edges from the taffeta with a pair of black handled scissors.

"Oh, no, ma'am. I mean Betsy. The tea's so warm and soothing at the end of a long day."

"No need to apologize. I rarely get to visit with another woman. My husband's not interested in sewing details. His attention lies strictly in seeing me wear the finished product." She laughed.

Laurabeth smiled. Had Ben noticed her pink cotton eyelet?

"So, off to the bedroom with you. I'm going to stay up awhile and get started on my pattern."

"What about Mr. Landers? Where will he sleep?"

"He'll bed down at the chuckwagon. The man longs for a good excuse to sit around and yarn with the boys." Betsy raised her eyebrows. "George won't admit the truth, but he spent too many years on the cattle trail to ever prefer a feather mattress over buffalo grass."

Within fifteen minutes, Laurabeth had washed her face and was pulling up a light quilt. She stretched her weary limbs, nestling into deep softness. Facing an open window, she again focused her thoughts upon the handsome young cowboy as moonbeams skipped across the waving prairie grasses.

"Where is he at this very moment?" she questioned the steady breeze. "Where are you, Ben Diamond?"

Just repeating his name caused her insides to tingle. Recalling his strong hands about her waist made her feel safe, more so than at any time since the terrible fire.

Her voice trailed into a whisper. "I wish Mary Michael were here." Laurabeth snugged the quilt around her shoulders. "I'd tell her about the two shooting stars melting into one, then traveling over the horizon. She would call the act *a heavenly sign*."

Closing her eyes, Laurabeth imagined writing her best friend a much-needed letter. Yet as her conscious thoughts drifted into slumber, she saw only Ben Diamond.

And dreamed of sharing the rest of her life with an XIT cowboy.

CHAPTER 19

Laurabeth awoke to bare clapboard walls bathed in sunlight. Sitting up, she rubbed her eyes. Betsy's side of the bed was empty.

Must be around 6 a.m.

Facing the open window, Laurabeth sniffed. For the first moment since leaving Galveston, the scent of moisture hung in the air. She missed the sweet, damp odor.

Smoothing back her hair, she scanned the room for her meager belongings. On the wall opposite the window, a row of wooden pegs supported her hat, undergarments and both dresses. In the far corner stood a marble topped washstand complete with a blue ceramic pitcher and basin, cake of lye soap, plus a white linen washcloth. Her hairbrush, ribbons and toilet water were neatly stowed on a nearby shelf. Betsy had insisted upon unpacking Laurabeth's things.

A sudden breeze stirred her next waking thought.

Ben Diamond.

How she'd hoped to eat last night's supper at the chuckwagon, but Betsy said the hands might stare. Were men on the Texas frontier like the stranger on the train?

Probably not. Most cowboys are just curious.

Yet Brett attempted to do much more than observe. She shivered.

Then the memory of Ben's gaze warmed her body. He'd simply looked. There wasn't any harm with a man *looking*. Women did the same. After all, closing one's eyes while meeting another person would be absurd.

Another strong breeze delivered the aroma of boiling coffee.

Breakfast. Ben would be there.

Laurabeth quickly dressed. After washing her face, she brushed her long curls then tied them back with a ribbon. The sun wasn't high enough to bother wearing a hat. With a grin, she rushed through the deserted house and out the front door. Clutching the sides of her dress, she scampered down the porch steps.

Seconds later, her grin vanished. Ben was nowhere in sight. The cowboys were already hard at work in the branding pens. Fifty yards beyond, Betsy rode beside Mr. Landers toward the south pasture.

She's lucky, spending time with the man she loves.

Behind the chuckwagon, Cookie hunched over a smoldering campfire. Twenty feet away, Useless sipped coffee from a tin cup. Mister and Mizz were hitched and ready to roll.

Laurabeth ran to her uncle, her voice suddenly breathless. "What the matter?" She pointed toward the mules.

"Morning Missy. You hungry? Folks around here eat breakfast victuals before sunup, so there ain't much left. I was fixing to come holler for you."

"Are we going somewhere?" Her heartbeat echoed between her ears.

"Don't you look right pretty."

"Then we're leaving?" She folded her arms.

Useless set down his cup. "I am. You ain't." He tugged his beard.

"Dag-nab-it." Cookie bellowed through a cloud of smoke and dust. He coughed, fanning the air with his hat. "Wind's fickle as a female."

Useless loudly cleared his throat.

Cookie glanced up, his face matching the hue of red-hot coals. "I mean … fickle as a female mule. Morning, Miss Appleby. Nobody had the good manners to tell me you were about." He glared at Useless. "Ain't you got a job to do?"

"I wouldn't be complaining about Mizz." Useless winked at Laurabeth. "Might hurt the animal's communication skills. She and Mister have been predicting rain for two days. Blue norther's coming. That's why the wind lays, then gusts from every direction."

"Don't care where the breeze blows as long as it stays clear of my fire. Some of us got to earn a living." Cookie jammed his hat down to his ears and nursed a small flame.

Laurabeth placed her hands on her hips. "Why are you leaving without me?"

"Now don't get all lathered up over nothing." Useless dug out his pipe and rapped the bowl against a boot heel, releasing a plug of gray ash. "I'm just delivering the rest of Charlie's load on up to the Spring Lake Division. Be back tomorrow evening."

A jumble of words and emotions clogged Laurabeth's throat. She didn't know how to respond. Where she was glad for more opportunities to see Ben, Uncle Eustus was family. And now, like Papa, her uncle was leaving her behind. She refused to let that happen again.

"I'm going with you."

Useless filled the bowl with tobacco. His jaw tightened. "Ain't room."

"What? The wagon's half empty."

"Listen, Missy." He spoke softly. "There ain't enough space for you *and* trouble. Charlie's killers are likely still hunting this load of goods. They might figure the payroll was also for Spring Lake. Better half the money than none."

"What if something terrible happens?" Her voice trembled. "What if you never—?" She turned away.

"Ain't no need to fret. The foreman's up to snuff on the recent shenanigans and will send out a posse if I'm late getting back. I'll keep my Winchester by my side. Mister and Mizz can smell danger a mile off. I'll guarantee those four-legged critters have saved my worthless hide more than once." Useless lit his pipe. "Did I ever tell of the night we roused a hungry grizzly?"

Laurabeth faced the south pasture, angry that he'd waste time telling stories when they may never see each other again. Passing through the far gate was a bright yellow carriage.

Or was it a wagon?

As the rig neared, she saw it was pulled by a team of dappled horses and carried two passengers. Betsy and Mr. Landers rode alongside.

"Well, I'll be plum jiggered." Useless paused in mid-story. "That's the dandiest buggy I ever saw."

Cookie abandoned his fire. "Ain't no buggy. That there's a buckboard."

"Got a folding top." Useless pointed. "No buckboard's got a folding top."

"No buggy's attached to a wagon bed." Cookie crossed his arms.

While the two men fussed, Laurabeth noticed how one of the passengers sported a white beard. The other wore an enormous hat resembling a bird's nest. "Cleo," Laurabeth shouted as the passengers rolled within earshot. "Colt."

Cleo boomed a greeting. "Well, hog tie and brand me. If that ain't the little gal from the train. Look Colt. She's Laurabeth Appleby."

When the strange rig halted, everyone spoke at once. Cleo leaped to the ground, smothering Laurabeth in a bear hug. "The world's sure enough a small place. Ain't that so, Colt?"

"Sure enough." He exited the driver's seat. "Howdy there, Miss Appleby."

Mr. Landers dismounted. "For you folks who don't know, this here's Colt Cole, the finest bronco buster this side of the Rio Grande." The foreman turned toward Cleo and tipped his hat. "I reckon you must be Mrs. Cole."

"You got the surname right, but I ain't nobody's Missus … yet." Cleo roared with delight. "I'm Cleopatra, Colt's big sister."

Laurabeth giggled. Cleo was *big* in every sense of the word.

Betsy hopped down from her mount. "Cookie? How about a cup of your delicious coffee?"

"Yes, ma'am. But first, me and Useless got to know something. Is this here fancy contraption a buckboard or buggy?"

"Buck-buggy." Cleo's grin spread the expanse of her face. "Got the comfort and protection of a buggy yet will tote a load the same as a buckboard. Colt and me invented the thing, didn't we, little brother?"

"We invented the thing."

Useless scratched his head. "Well, I'll be plum jiggered."

Cookie prepared more coffee, while Betsy handed out cups. Laurabeth introduced her uncle to Cleo and Colt, then apprised the pair of her journey from Ft. Worth to Colorado City and on to the Yellow Houses. She told about hiding inside One-Eared Charlie's freight wagon, and his murder by the so-called Comanches.

Cleo nodded. "You're lucky Useless come along. A lady can't trust the traveling public these days, even when she's a stowaway."

After coffee was poured, everyone continued to visit. Laurabeth secretly scanned the area for Ben. He wasn't in any of the branding pens, and the corrals weren't in sight of the chuck wagon. Perhaps he rode the range, doing whatever cowboys did out there.

She sighed.

Ben Diamond was a fast-fading memory.

Cleo's commanding voice directed Laurabeth's attention back to the group. "Now don't nobody get the wrong idea. I ain't no official doctor like Daddy, but he taught me all the medicine a body needs to know. So I said to Colt ... little brother, if you desire my healing hands out on the frontier, I insist upon traveling in comfort and safety. A dignified lady shouldn't have to ride no bumpy stage nor thief-infested train."

Cookie refilled Cleo's cup. He grinned, revealing no more than a dozen teeth. "I'm glad you're here, ma'am. I ain't hardly got time to cook, much less doctor the boys."

"He means *torture* the boys," Useless said.

Everyone laughed.

Cookie grunted. "Gives me more time for cooking." He set down the coffeepot. "Miss Cleopatra? I'd like to hear more about this dandy yellow buck-buggy."

With the enthusiasm of a Sunday circuit rider, Cleo preached about the folding cloth top and comfortable inner spring seat. Since she was named after royalty, she'd covered the seat with an appropriate purple, velvet fabric. Cleo explained how Colt needed a place to carry his tack and equipment, so they'd added the wagon bed behind the weatherproof buggy shell.

During a rare pause, Mr. Landers spoke. "Did you folks notice anybody else kicking up dust along the XIT road?"

"Saw fresh tracks," Colt replied.

"How many horses?" Useless wiped his brow.

"Two, but only one rider. Tracks showed he was moving fast."

Useless frowned. "What about Old Man Singer? Did you stop at his place?"

"Watered the team at the lake but didn't go around far enough to see the store.

"Colt was in a hurry to get on up here, weren't you, Little Brother?"

He agreed. "Didn't want to keep them wild horses waiting."

The talk turned to horse training as the sun rose higher, heating the already parched landscape. Useless participated while his eyes scanned the circumference of the vast plain. After a final cup of coffee, he retreated toward his wagon, claiming he needed to check the mules' rigging before pulling out for Spring Lake.

Laurabeth followed.

"Come to tell Mister and Mizz goodbye?"

She patted the animals' soft noses. "I saw you watching the horizon, as you did the day we climbed the caprock."

Useless raised an eyebrow. "We Applebys don't miss a trick." He chuckled. "Reckon an old Texas Ranger never retires."

"I've decided to stay here where it's safe." She faced her uncle. "No need to worry about me."

"We're sensible too."

She threw her arms around his neck. He looked so much like Papa, Laurabeth imagined having him back. "Please be careful. We Applebys aren't very good at that."

"I reckon we'll have to change our ways."

Ten minutes later, Laurabeth stood frozen, watching Mister and Mizz plod north toward Spring Lake. True to his word, she'd watched her uncle stow his rifle within arm's reach, which didn't change the fact her only kin was heading into possible danger. Papa never knew for certain when he might sail into the jaws of a powerful Gulf storm.

A gnawing ache filled her stomach with emptiness. Life atop the plains was as unpredictable as life on the ocean. At least Cleo and Colt had arrived.

And Ben?

The memory of his clear blue eyes eased the pain in her middle.

"Useless will be fine." Three feet away, Betsy sat astride her horse. "I didn't mean to startle you, but that man leads a charmed life. Could be because he was a Ranger. Or perhaps his stories keep him safe."

"His stories?"

"If your uncle was ever captured by outlaws, he'd talk them to death. And now that I've met Cleo, well ..."

Laurabeth met Betsy's wide smile with her own. "If Cleo and my uncle ever join forces, entire murderous bands will surrender without a shot fired."

The smiles broke into laughter.

Betsy continued. "I've invited Cleo to stay at the ranch house. Cookie's delivering her bag. Would you be kind enough to help her unpack?"

"Of course." Laurabeth remembered Cleo's ragged snoring. "Where will she sleep?"

"She'll share the bedroom with you. I'll stretch out on a cot in the kitchen." Betsy nudged her mount forward. "I need to ride back out to the south pasture with George and count newborn calves. We'll eat with the boys today, so dinner's at the chuckwagon, twelve o'clock sharp."

The smoky aroma of frying beef whipped into the ranch house bedroom through an open window. "That smell will start your innards to humming." Cleo rubbed her stomach. "What time's dinner?"

"Noon." Laurabeth peered outside, envisioning a shared meal with Ben. "We get to eat at the chuckwagon. Isn't that wonderful?"

"Eating anyplace where Colt and me ain't cooking is wonderful. Mama couldn't cook worth nothin'. Can you believe that little woman had the gall to teach both her offspring." Cleo pulled a wad of clothes out of a large carpetbag. "Remember my bag that got stole? The one decorated with stuffed robins?"

Half-listening, Laurabeth nodded.

"Couldn't locate an exact replica, so I bought this one adorned with chickens. Rhode Island Reds. Not life sized, but ain't they pretty? 'Bout the same color as robins, so my new bag almost matches my hat."

"Robins are nice." Laurabeth recalled the chip pile incident.

What if Ben is still too embarrassed to speak?

"Reckon I can hang my hat and dresses on those pegs, right beside your things." Cleo shook her bag upside down to empty the remaining contents.

Laurabeth sat at the foot of the bed.

Even if Ben talks, how will I get to spend much time with him?

She glanced at Cleo. "I suppose you can hang your hat and dresses next to my things.

"Ain't that what I just said?" Cleo hung the clothes and removed her hat. Mounds of dark hair sprang free. "I'm glad them robins ain't real. There'd be droppings all over my fancy straw." She laughed heartily. "And everybody knows what kind of mess chickens make."

"Chickens are nice too."

Cleo plopped down beside Laurabeth. "Is something bothering you? Another stranger?"

"He might as well be." Laurabeth lowered her head, drew in a deep breath and slowly released it. "His name is Ben," she began, telling about first seeing him. How her initial feelings were reinforced by his steady gentleness while helping her down from the wagon. Then came the magic meeting of their eyes, followed by his embarrassing fall and how she'd reacted. "What if he's still upset and won't talk?"

Cleo's chin rested between her massive palms. Without a word, she stood and paced the length of the room. "Tripping over that shovel was surely unfortunate."

"Then why did I laugh?"

"'Cause those sorts of accidents are so danged funny." Cleo hooted. "Awh, honey, you had to have been six feet under not to pop a giggle. He'll get over the embarrassment. Just lost a little false pride. The male species is born with way too much of that nonsense. Don't hurt none of 'em to lose a little. Besides, pride ain't the issue."

Laurabeth swallowed hard. "What is?"

"Matters of the heart. Most men ain't real bright when love's involved. But, honey, a man's eyes never lie. Since

I'm a betting woman, I'd wager Ben's smart enough to figure out the truth."

"The truth?"

"The boy knows he's sprawled head over heels into something deeper than a stack of stinky old cow pies."

Laurabeth squinted her brow. "Then Ben wants to spend time with me?"

"Yes'm. He just don't know how. All he needs is the right opportunity."

"That could take years."

"Not with a little encouragement."

"Encouragement?" Laurabeth felt her mood brighten.

Cleo's lips parted into a mischievous grin. "How 'bout you two take a drive in my fancy yellow buck-buggy?"

"Oh, Cleo, that would be wonderful." The excited response tumbled from Laurabeth's mouth. "When?"

"This evening, I'll wager." She paused. "But like me, you've got to be willing to gamble."

"Why?"

"'Cause, honey, the only way to win a man like Ben Diamond is to bet your whole heart."

CHAPTER 20

Halting his mount, Ben scooted back in the saddle and stretched his tired legs. Throughout the night watch, the breeze remained steady and the remuda calm. An hour before dawn, the wind died altogether, resurrecting into warm gusts as the sun rose. By midmorning, he kept having to snug down his hat. It had already blown off his head twice.

Since his fight with Jake Crow outside the feed shed, Ben hadn't seen the other wrangler. Jake was supposed to take the shift at first light, but with yesterday being payday, the troublemaker was likely somewhere sleeping off too much whisky. The cowboy who'd finally relieved Ben for breakfast was tightlipped concerning Jake's absence. "That one ain't got the makings for ranch work," was all the man said.

Sitting square in his saddle, Ben clicked his horse into motion, riding another circle around the remuda. A deep growl vibrated his empty stomach. He should've eaten breakfast.

Breakfast.

Laurabeth wasn't there.

Throughout the lonely night, he'd pictured her sparkling, brown eyes. Recalled her sweet, girlish giggle.

He couldn't blame her for laughing. Falling into the chip pile was funny. He would've reacted the same.

Initially, he was relieved with her absence. Yet after loading his plate with biscuits and gravy, he imagined his hands around her delicate waist. Recalled her angelic smell. Disappointment stabbed his heart, which made swallowing a single bite impossible.

When Cookie noticed Ben wasn't eating, he mumbled about the dry weather causing stopped up innards, then ordered the boy swallow a healthy swig of castor oil and rest a couple of hours. Instead of resting, Ben rode back to the remuda to finish Jake's shift ... and think.

"Ain't nothin' that tastes worse to a man than castor oil," Ben informed his mount. "And ain't nothin' that confuses a man more than a beautiful girl. Be glad you're a horse."

After another round, Mr. Landers and a cowboy rode into view. The cowboy cantered to the opposite side of the herd.

"Everything under control, son?" Mr. Landers reined to a stop.

"Yes, sir." Ben wondered why the cowboy was there.

The foreman wiped his brow with a red bandana and frowned. "Ain't seen a glimpse of Jake Crow. So for the time being, the remuda's on its own."

Cold sweat drops pooled at the base of Ben's neck. His muscles tightened. Word must've leaked about his pa. Because of Jake, they'd both be fired.

The boss continued. "I've had a gut full of Crow's shenanigans. I reckon you feel the same."

"Yes, sir."

"You've done a good job, son, and deserve a better partner. I'll see what I can do."

"Thank you." A wave of relief washed over Ben. His confused heart longings had turned his mind to mush, making him leap to false conclusions. In the future, he'd be more levelheaded. Still, he was puzzled about Mr. Landers's plans.

"Ever hear of a man named Colt Cole?"

"Hasn't everyone? He's that broncobuster who never gets throwed."

The foreman chuckled. "He's famous 'round these parts for good reason. Most breakers only last a few years 'cause they get plum shook apart. Colt's been on the job for a decade. He must have rawhide for bones."

"Do you know him?"

"Never laid eyes on the man till this morning."

"He's here?" Ben's jaw dropped.

"Colt and his sister, Cleo, traveled all the way from Fort Worth in a contraption they call a buck-buggy. Bright yellow. Most unusual wagon you ever saw. Headquarters is paying him two dollars a head to break the more dogged critters in this herd of raw mustangs."

Ben nodded, having dealt daily with the same stubborn horses. He'd never heard of a buck-buggy nor any wagon painted yellow.

"As part of the deal, the ranch provides Colt an assistant. After the way you've handled these animals, I reckon you're the best man for the job. What do you think?"

A full grin occupied Ben's face.

"Good." Mr. Landers signaled the cowboy with his hat. "We'll cut and deliver the renegades over to Colt. He wants to start directly, so don't wait on dinner. Hightail into camp for a quick bite of whatever Cookie's done fixed, then meet Colt at the corrals."

"What about the rest of the remuda?"

"They won't wander far. Check on 'em about sunset. If you miss supper, I'll have Cookie hold you a plate. Try to get some rest before the midnight watch." The boss sighed. "I hate to assign double duty, son, but Crow has left us in a bad way."

Ben made a beeline for the chuckwagon. What an honor to work with Colt Cole. Earning a job as an official cowhand crept closer with each passing day.

Only after Ben gulped down dinner and rode toward the corrals did he allow himself to think about Laurabeth. Eating early ruined any opportunity for seeing her at the chuckwagon. Even so, there was no guarantee she'd pay attention to him, what with all the boys standing around gawking. He'd best forget her. Bronco busting was dangerous business. A distracted man might finish his career sleeping in a pine box.

Topping a slight rise, Ben spotted two corrals with rail fences. The larger, constructed around a windmill, already held the problem horses. The smaller was where the breaking would take place. A lanky, white bearded cowboy dressed in long leather chaps hung tack on a top rail. A coil of rope was slung over his shoulder.

"Howdy." Ben slid out of the saddle and extended his right hand. "My name's Ben Diamond. Are you Mr. Cole?"

"Reckon somebody's got to be." Colt gripped Ben's hand with a firm shake. "Just call me Colt."

"Yes, sir, Mr. Colt."

The breaker smiled, then selected a pair of short shank spurs. "I appreciate the help, Ben. While I strap on these *gentle reminders*, you grab a lasso. Then we'd best get started."

Instantly, Ben admired Colt's easy ways. Blunt spurs rather than sharpened rowels indicated a breaker who cared about the animal's welfare.

With lassos in hand, the two men mounted and rode into the large corral. Colt pointed to a feisty bay. "How 'bout starting with that one? Looks to be the roughest in the bunch."

Ben nodded. The man's judgment of horseflesh was a dead aim.

Colt lowered his voice. "Reckon you can sneak in and slip a loop over that bronc's head?"

Hiding the rope behind his back, Ben urged his mount into the center of the herd. The horses were used to him and didn't shy. In one fluid motion, Ben swung the rope and fired a perfect circle, hitting his mark. The bay leapt into the air.

"Good job, pardner." Colt charged into the scattering herd and flung a second loop. The bay lunged and resisted but had little choice than to be dragged into the smaller corral.

"Hitch him up short to that snubbing post," Colt instructed, "so he can't jerk his head. I'll dismount and slip a bridle on him."

In seconds, the bridle was secure. Even though the horse couldn't rear, his eyes remained wild, muscles tense.

Then Colt did something unexpected.

From his saddlebag, the breaker produced a swath of soft, black cloth and blindfolded the anxious animal. The bay relaxed.

"He ain't scared of what he can't see." Colt spoke casually. "I'll fasten on a saddle while you hold the reins taut. When I release the ropes, he'll think he's still tied."

With the saddle secured, Colt untied and coiled the lassos. "Ready to commence with some fun?"

"Anytime." Ben thought the fun had already started.

"Keep a hold while I climb on." Colt stepped into the left stirrup and swung a leg over. The bay perked his ears yet remained still. "Now hand me the reins and git over to the fence." He winked. "Show's about to begin."

Perched upon the top rail, Ben had a front row seat. For an instant, he dreamed about sharing this exciting moment with Laurabeth but quickly forced the scene from his mind.

Still holding the reins, Colt adjusted his hat and squirmed deep into the saddle. With his free hand, he untied the blindfold. Two seconds passed, and nothing happened.

Then the bay exploded into action.

Colt gripped hard with his thighs as the animal lowered his head and sprang straight into the air. With a tremendous jerk, the bronco rounded his back. The breaker flew above the saddle though didn't lose his seat. Landing on stiff legs, the bay jerked, jumped, and rounded again, this time landing sideways. Colt bounced hard, yet kept his balance, holding his posture perfectly upright.

"Ride 'em," Ben hollered. Time and again, the bay repeated his bucking routine, landing sideways then backward and forward.

When the horse tired, Colt lightly pressed his spurs into the animal's flanks. With a loud snort, the bronco doubled with renewed energy, rearing and plunging more viciously than before. The breaker continued using his spurs until the animal slowed into exhaustion.

Colt dismounted, then stroked the bay's sweat-drenched neck. He motioned for Ben to join him. "Take our new friend on a little jaunt around the corral while he's too tuckered to fight. Tomorrow, we'll see what he learned."

"How many days till he's fully broke?" Ben swung into the saddle.

"Usually takes three. Four or five for a spirited critter like this one."

As Ben trotted the bronco around the corral's perimeter, images of Laurabeth crept back into his mind. "I must stop thinking about her," he whispered to the bay. "I've a job to do. A chance to prove myself." Although, the harder his brain tried to forget, the more his heart ached to remember.

Even though the next mustang fought with great effort, the horse was subdued in less time. Gradually, the two men developed a system, quickening their pace. Ben learned, then mastered, each new task with silent gusto.

As the afternoon waned, the wind increased, whirling a layer of fine prairie dust into the cloudless sky.

"I'm done in." Colt took a deep breath as the sixth bronco was released into the large corral. He glanced west at a hazy sun. "Reckon supper's still a good hour away. Probably ought to tackle one more."

"I'd like to try." The perilous words escaped from Ben's lips before he had time to stop them.

The breaker stroked his beard, then unstrapped his spurs. "I'd be most obliged." He handed them to Ben.

A stout roan was roped, saddled, and blindfolded.

"Trust your leg grip and balance." Colt stood close as Ben climbed on. The nervous animal was already breathing hard.

"Yes, sir."

"Keep your head, and you'll do fine." Colt handed over the reins and backed toward the fence.

Gathering courage, Ben tightly clamped his legs, untied the blindfold and let it fall. The bronco laid his ears back, dropped to his knees then shot skyward. Ben flew high above the saddle. With a loud pop, his backside slammed down against hard leather. Before he could gain another hold, a powerful buck catapulted him over the roan's head. Ben sat stunned in a cloud of dust.

Hoots of laughter echoed from the fence. "Looks like you've attracted an audience." Colt offered a hand up. "The crew riding in from the east pasture must've heard the ruckus. Suppose they couldn't resist the show."

Ben stood and brushed off his chaps. "Then let's give 'em some real entertainment."

Colt nodded. "Reckon I'll go grab a rope."

As the roan was again caught and blindfolded, the crowd grew. Shouts of *breaker-boy* and *tenderfoot* only made Ben more determined to ride the mustang.

"Sit easy," Colt whispered. "Keep your spine straight, not stiff. Pretend you ain't got a backbone."

Like before, the bronco leaped high into the air. Ben bounced above the saddle, then landed loose, keeping his balance. The roan kicked and plunged, twisting from side to side.

"Gonna eat dirt," yelled a cowboy.

"Or something worse," shouted another.

Ben hung on for what seemed an eternity. The wild horse began to weaken.

"Use your spurs," bellowed an unfamiliar female voice. "Make a believer outta that ornery critter."

Glancing toward the fence, Ben spied the bright yellow buck-buggy. A large woman stood barefoot atop the driver's seat, waving her arms and cheering. She had to be Cleo. Beside her was the beautiful smiling girl.

Laurabeth.

The roan lunged with a powerful jerk. Surrounded by sky, Ben crashed into a fresh pile of horse droppings. The cowboys whooped in delight.

"Lost your concentration's all." Colt's voice was relaxed. "Happens to the best of men."

Ben stood on wobbly legs and hung his head. Searing pain pulsed from his left ankle. This fall was more embarrassing than the chip pile.

"Look at me, son." Colt's grey eyes twinkled. "That was a mighty fine ride. Getting dumped is part of the learning. Usually hurts a man's pride more than his bones."

A sudden determination boiled deep within Ben's gut. "Show's not over," he whispered. "This ain't the end."

The roan was readied for a third time. Ignoring his throbbing ankle, Ben mounted.

"Grip tight with your legs between each bounce," Colt said, "if only for a second. That's the secret from getting throwed."

Clutching the reins, Ben reached for the blindfold. The crowd hushed. Turning his head toward the fence he spied Laurabeth. Once again, their eyes met. He tipped his hat and dropped the blindfold.

The wild bronco bolted upward with renewed vigor. Committed to victory, Ben focused upon each twist and turn, envisioning what would happen next. Within three minutes, the roan weakened and gave up the fight. Applying spurs wasn't necessary.

"He done the impossible," Cleo roared. "That boy is pure grit."

The cowboys whooped in agreement as the supper bell clanged. With shouts of *chuck* and *grub's on* they charged their mounts toward the chuckwagon.

Ben patted the exhausted bronco and dismounted, being careful not to place much weight on his hurt ankle. Out of the corner of his eye, he spied the yellow buck-buggy. Why hadn't Laurabeth gone to supper?

"Fine job, son. Ain't a man around could've done better." Colt unsaddled the roan and shooed him in with the other horses. "I'd like you to meet my sister." Both men headed toward the buck-buggy.

"Looks like you're favoring an ankle," Cleo called, still perched atop the seat. "Best smear on some bear grease. Ain't nothing any better for sprains than bear grease, huh, little brother?"

"Ain't nothing any better." Colt grinned. "This here's my sister, Cleo, who's also my doctor. I reckon you've already met Miss Appleby."

Ben tipped his hat and nodded.

Laurabeth returned his greeting with a smile. "I enjoyed watching you ride."

"Thank you, ma'am." Ben tipped and nodded again.

Colt cuffed Ben on his shoulder. "Reckon we'd best mount up and mosey over to supper. I'm starved."

"Not so fast." Cleo hopped down from the velvet seat. "Ben ain't moseying nowhere that involves climbing into a saddle. Needs to keep his weight off that ankle till tomorrow."

"The boy's hungry," Colt protested.

"I appreciate your concern ma'am, but I'm fine." Ben took a step and grimaced.

Cleo crossed her thick arms and glared at Colt. "You know arguing with a doctor ain't healthy. I reckon Ben can drive this here buck-buggy to supper. I'll ride his horse."

"But, Miss Cleo, ma'am—?"

"Don't you argue with no doctor, neither."

Ben removed his hat, passing it from hand to hand. "The boss wants me to check on the rest of the remuda before sunset. Plus, I gotta pick up a bucket of grain. Cookie's saving me a plate."

"Then the buck-buggy's perfect," Cleo boomed. "And there's a sack of oats in the back, along with a bucket. I'll bet Laurabeth would enjoy an evening's ride in a fine rig. Ain't that right, honey?"

"Y ... yes. That would be wonderful."

"Then everything's settled. I'll make sure Cookie saves two plates."

"I'll repay the feed, ma'am." Ben replaced his hat.

"No need. You earned a bonus helping Colt." Cleo marched barefoot toward Ben's mount. "Takes skill to ride a horse in a dress, don't you agree, little brother?"

Colt wagged his head. "Whatever you say."

CHAPTER 21

Brett Castle crouched behind the grassy rim of Yellow House Canyon, watching the unusual yellow buggy head toward the south pasture.

He'd never seen a more useful rig.

Under normal circumstances, he'd meet the owner and learn about the manufacturer. Then he'd order one for himself and a dozen more for the mercantile to sell at a handsome profit. However, present circumstances were far from normal. News concerning the fates of One-Eared Charlie and El Cuchillo would soon trickle into Colorado City.

Vernon Abbot would grow suspicious.

Sitting back on his haunches, Brett scowled, recalling his own intentions to become a lawyer. His plan was to save Colorado City from Abbot's greedy clutches, plus get rich in the process. After Brett argued the cost benefits of having an attorney in the family, his father agreed. So Brett traveled east to attend St. Louis Law College.

During his first year, he fell in love with a local socialite, Ivory Cane—the youngest child of a wealthy railroad magnate. The girl was beautiful and spoiled with an unquenchable desire for expensive gifts. Since extravagance reaped sensual rewards, Brett spent handsomely.

Within six months, his desire to be with Ivory replaced his dream to best Vernon Abbott. Brett abandoned his studies. For all he cared, Colorado City could wither in the Texas heat. Though when grades were released, his father refused to send more money. So Brett determined to give Ivory a gift he'd never offered any other woman.

His heart.

The night he proposed, Ivory merely laughed. The next day, she casually dropped him, adopting a new lover with much deeper pockets.

Filled with hurt and rage, Brett vowed to spread the word about Ivory's promiscuous ways. In return, she threatened to accuse him of rape, a crime that would leave a bankrupt outsider swinging from a rope. No jury would disbelieve the daughter of a prominent St. Louis businessman.

Broken and bitter, Brett headed back to Colorado City to work hard and reclaim his father's respect. He pledged to never give his heart to another woman, to allow her to control him, and to destroy his financial dreams. In the future, he'd use women to *his* advantage.

Brett Castle would be the one in power. No one would deny him money ... or love.

A gusty breeze forced his attention to the job at hand. He gazed over the parched landscape. The girl in the strange buggy was no longer in sight.

"My losing the mercantile at poker was *her* fault." Disappointment spewed from his lips. "She holds no regard for a man's kindness. Therefore, I must teach her the proper gratitude."

He'd watched the ranch house throughout the day from the same hidden location. She'd ventured outside twice, though never unescorted. Spending time alone with her wouldn't prove easy, yet he'd find a way.

"Tonight," he muttered. "Gotta happen tonight."

Scooting below the rim, he stood and returned to where his horses were tethered. Grabbing whiskey from his saddlebags, he uncorked the bottle, took a long swig, and considered his options. Convincing Abbott to extend payback time wasn't hard. Brett would simply up the ante, taking advantage of the man's natural greed.

Marrying the girl was the difficult task. His reputation *and* neck were at stake.

Spying the small trunk tied behind his saddle, he recalled the ranch payroll. His mind formed an instant plan. "Payday for the Yellow House Division was yesterday," he whispered. "I need someone new to bribe."

For the past couple of years, mercantile freighters yarned about a crumbling adobe shack called Hell's Pit, located southwest of the XIT boundary on Sulphur Draw. The lawless establishment was where men from the Texas and New Mexico territories met to drink and gamble. A place where gold and gunpowder spoke louder than words.

Raising the bottle to his lips, Brett gulped more whiskey.

As soon as darkness enveloped the prairie, he'd hide the extra horse and ride to Hell's Pit. Finding an already penniless cowboy was gravy.

Brett Castle would get exactly what he wanted ... this time.

CHAPTER 22

Laurabeth leaned back into the buck-buggy's plush seat, then slid moist hands beneath the folds of her pink eyelet. "Such a beautiful evening," she stated for the third time.

Ben nodded and tipped his hat, also for the third time. He remained silent.

Drawing a deep breath, she remembered Cleo's advice about taking a gamble. "I love the orange glow of the prairie at sunset. Sure makes for a beautiful evening. Don't you agree?"

Silence.

"So ... you *don't* agree the evening's beautiful?"

"No, ma'am. I mean, y ... yes, ma'am." Ben tipped his hat again.

"Well, I'll be plum jiggered." Laurabeth giggled. "You *can* talk." Since leaving the corrals, he'd not uttered a single word, but focused straight ahead, keeping a firm grip on the buck-buggy's reins."

"Yes, ma'am."

"Dear me." Laurabeth raised her eyebrows. "I believe *yes* and *ma'am* are the only two words you have left. That bronco must've bucked the rest of your speech right out of your mouth."

Facing her, Ben's cheeks crinkled into a crooked grin. "Reckon I don't know what to say to a lady who's prettier than any evening ever thought about being."

"Thank you. I ..." Laurabeth's mind went blank. Her face grew hot.

He continued. "This is one bad drought. Sure be glad when it breaks."

"My Uncle Eustus swears his mules are predicting rain. A little moisture would be nice."

"No, ma'am. A *lot* of moisture would be nice."

They both laughed.

Laurabeth placed her hands in her lap. "Cleo agrees. She says we need more than a thunderstorm or two. We need a wet spell."

As they topped a slight rise, the lazy remuda came into view. Four-legged shadows followed each grazing animal, producing elongated shapes. A fireball sun rested atop the western horizon.

"The horses remind me of little sailboats on the Gulf of Mexico," Laurabeth stated softly, "their legs casting mast-like shadows."

Ben reined the buck-buggy to a gentle stop. "I've never seen a sailboat, 'cept in pictures. Nor have I ever spied the Gulf." He looked at Laurabeth. "I reckon that traveling with your uncle takes you to a lot of different locations."

"No. Yes." Her words melted into silence as she met Ben's gaze. Ocean calm pooled within his eyes.

"Well, how about that." Ben grinned. "I'm afraid *no* and *yes* are the only words *you* have left.

They laughed again.

Laurabeth spoke easily. "I've visited many places, but not with Uncle Eustus. I sailed with my parents. My father was a sea captain."

And then with words resembling the effortless patter of summer rain, she told about her mother's illness and her father's ship going down—about Saint Mary's Orphan Asylum, Sister Mary Michael, and how God's grace enabled the finding of her uncle.

"You're an orphan too," Ben whispered. Releasing the buck-buggy's reins, he reached over and squeezed her hand. The sun dipped below the rim of the prairie.

Laurabeth's heart pounded, the phrase *you're an orphan too* echoing between beats.

A sudden whinny trumpeted through the dusk. Twenty yards away stood the most magnificent blue stallion Laurabeth had ever seen.

"His name is Storm," Ben proudly stated. "I had a feeling he'd come around. Watch this."

Ben slowly climbed down from the seat and stepped to the buck-buggy's rear. Taking the bucket, he filled it with grain. Placing weight on his good ankle, he inched toward Storm. The stallion snorted, reared twice, then settled. Ben emptied the grain on the ground and returned.

"Why won't he eat," Laurabeth whispered. "Isn't he hungry?"

Yet before Ben could reply, she saw the golden mare.

He matched Laurabeth's whisper. "I reckon Storm's letting her eat first. She's been feeling poorly."

No other animals in the remuda approached while the horses ate. Ben and Laurabeth watched in shared awe until both mustangs faded into the dusk. Then Ben clicked the team into motion for the return trip.

Laurabeth hoped he'd squeeze her hand again, perhaps hold it. But even if he didn't, the evening was a wonderful experience. Watching him interact with the blue stallion made her tingle. So while the buck-buggy rattled back toward the ranch house, questions about this caring cowboy bounced inside her head, all begging for answers.

"You said you're also an orphan?" Laurabeth faced him. "Do you remember your parents?"

"I never knew them."

"I'm sorry. Do you know anything about them?"

Silence.

"I'll declare." She laughed. "Seems like your speech has disappeared again. I'll bet your mother had this trouble with your father."

Ben cleared his throat, yet no words came.

More silence.

An all too familiar tightness gripped Laurabeth's middle. Surely, she'd asked nothing offensive. Like her, he probably still longed for his family, perhaps even hurt for them. Maybe her saying something positive would help. A lighthearted phrase to remind him of his folks.

"I'll bet you're just like your parents," she boldly stated, "especially your father."

The heavy dusk thickened into night.

An eternity passed.

Ben kept both eyes fixed on the road ahead. He didn't utter a sound.

What had she done to offend him? What had she said?

For some unexplained reason he'd turned to stone.

Laurabeth faced forward. A single tear escaped. She quickly wiped it, refusing to embarrass herself by crying in his presence.

When they reached the ranch house, she hopped out of the buck-buggy. Without a word, she scampered onto the porch and through the front entrance.

Luckily, no one was there.

Safely inside, she didn't try to hide her tears ... this time.

CHAPTER 23

The crumbling adobe shack known as Hell's Pit wasn't hard to locate on such a bright night. Brett Castle dismounted and tied his horse to the rickety hitching rail, noting that three other mounts wore the XIT brand. He laughed out loud as a gusty southeast wind kicked dirt into his face. This part of his plan was effortless.

His laugh melted into a satisfied smirk considering the genius of his actions. But then an image of the beautiful girl flashed across his memory, quickening his pulse.

He frowned.

After seeing her with that young cowboy, Brett wanted her more than ever.

Reaching inside his britches' pocket, Brett fingered five twenty-dollar gold pieces he'd borrowed from the mercantile's safe.

The smirk returned.

Finding a dishonest and dissatisfied cowboy in this godforsaken place wouldn't take long—one who could be bribed into performing a little dirty work.

The whine of rusty hinges announced Brett's entrance into a dimly lit room. Atop a dirt floor, two makeshift tables were surrounded by a dozen or more men, the air thick with tobacco smoke. Still, the entire establishment reeked of stale liquor, coal oil, and sweat.

Talking and movement ceased.

"Name's Red." A burly, rusty-bearded man aimed a sawed-off shotgun in Brett's direction. "What's your business?"

"Play poker, drink whiskey." Brett studied his surroundings. Lamplight flickered about the shot up remains of what was once the bar. In the shadows, an enormous rattlesnake skin hung from a low rafter.

"Rules ain't hard." Red kept his gun pointed. "Strangers sit at my table. Play till they run outta money. Then ride back where they came from."

Brett nodded.

Red continued. "Ain't no loans from other players. No IOU's, neither. Drink your own whisky. Ask no questions." The big man smiled. "And if I get an inkling you're a lawman, you'll end up same as that rattler who tried to take up housekeeping."

"Fair enough." Brett was certain he'd seen several of these men on wanted posters, especially Red. Since the outlaw seemed to be in charge of Hell's Pit, was he also the devil? The thought hit Brett as funny, though he dared not laugh.

Not yet.

During the first hand, Brett realized an XIT cowboy sat next to him. Two players across the table—also XIT hands—called the man Jake. They kept teasing him about getting beat up by a mare and a kid—said a rumor predicted Jake's likely dismissal.

"Ain't no dumb animal gonna best me ever again." Jake emptied the remains of a bottle down his throat, then slammed a handful of coins onto the table. "I'll kill that sorry excuse for horseflesh. The kid too."

Laughter scooted around the table. Someone called.

"Full house." Red racked in his winnings as the other players threw down their cards.

During the next hand, Brett raised the pot until he was certain Jake surrendered the remainder of his pay. Red accused Brett of bluffing, increasing the pot even more. The other players folded. Brett matched the raise with what appeared to be his last dollar, then called. Even though he held the winning hand, he dropped his cards in defeat. The scheme worked perfectly.

"I believe time's come for you two losers to be on your merry way." Red slid his shotgun from beneath the table. "Though feel free to join us the next time gold jingles in your pockets." He shook with laughter.

Outside, the wind had risen even more. Jake shouted strings of curses about his losses and the cowboys who'd made fun of him.

Brett opened a saddlebag and offered Jake a new bottle. "I ain't got no use for big outfits like the XIT."

Jake removed the cork and swallowed a healthy gulp. "They're too high and mighty to recognize a man's true worth. I hate the whole lot of 'em."

Between his thumb and forefinger, Brett held a shiny gold piece, allowing it to glisten in the moonlight. "How'd you like to earn a fast twenty, plus get revenge on the XIT?"

"What do you care?" Jake took another drink. "You don't work for that crowd."

"Personal reasons. And because they take advantage of decent folks like us."

Jake studied the coin. "What do I need to do?"

"Start a small grass fire in the south pasture later tonight. Come morning, the Yellow House Division will only be a bad memory."

"What if I refuse?"

"The next cowboy won't. And he'll be twenty dollars richer."

After another sip, Jake reached for the coin. Brett jerked the gold piece away, slipping it back inside his pocket. He handed Jake a box of matches. "Meet me at dawn at that hidden offshoot in Yellow House Canyon near the south pasture. You'll get your money then."

As Brett rode back toward the ranch, he chuckled at his new partner's stupidity in believing he'd get paid. In less than three hours, the fire would rage. Then everyone would rush hell-bent-for-leather to defeat the flames.

"An impossible task in this steady gale." Speaking aloud gave Brett power. "What with all the vegetation so brittle."

He chuckled again, realizing how everything in the fire's path would be destroyed, including the ranch house and outbuildings. The episode also meant an abundance of new lumber and supplies for the mercantile to sell.

Brett reached behind his back and stroked the little trunk. The final stage of his plan energized him most. In all the confusion, he'd have ample opportunity to grab the girl. Plenty of time to return her precious belongings.

And then a plaguing thought made his muscles ache, a reoccurring idea refusing to vacate his mind. What—if after all he'd done for her—she still refused to marry him?

The solution remained. He'd finish what *she* began back in Colorado City.

"The girl still owes me."

Brett urged his mount into a trot.

If need be, the fire provided a convenient accident, the intense heat destroying any incriminating evidence.

CHAPTER 24

Gripping the reins tighter, Ben continued his dutiful circling of the remuda. Throughout the moonlit wee hours, he'd eyed the distant ranch house. A beautiful girl named Laurabeth Appleby slept inside.

His stomach churned.

She probably hated him now.

"Oh God ... help me know what to do."

The unexpected prayer slipped out of Ben's mouth. Laurabeth's mention of her strong faith made him remember his, recalling the passion of his belief. Of late, he'd not sought heavenly help, yet he knew God was always with him.

Waiting.

Watching.

Listening.

Ben spoke skyward. "Why couldn't I answer her questions? I wanted to, yet the words stuck in my throat."

A strong wind gust whipped the rim of his hat as lightening crackled across the sky. He'd noticed the low cloud bank blowing in from the southeast.

The horses pricked up their ears.

"Easy."

Ben dismounted, aware of not placing too much weight on his sprained ankle. He tightened the saddle's cinch and frowned. A brewing storm was no time to be upset over a girl. He must concentrate on the job at hand. The ranch needed rain, not a stampede. If the remuda ran, the cattle would follow.

Lightening flashed again as Ben remounted. The remuda swung their heads, then moved into a nervous mill, as if performing a circular dance.

"Easy now. Ain't nothing but a little harmless lightening."

As hard as Ben tried to redirect his thoughts, they kept returning to his conversation with Laurabeth ... or rather his lack of a verbal response. An empty queasiness occupied his entire being. More worrisome than the approaching storm was the tear he'd noticed sliding down her cheek.

He should've stopped the rig.

Held her in his arms.

Told her about his past.

Yet didn't.

Couldn't.

And now the time for truth had passed.

He released a heavy sigh.

The damage was done.

Fingers of lightening splintered across the sky, followed by low rumbles of thunder.

The dance grew more anxious.

"I said, easy." Ben crammed his hat on tighter. The hands snoring at headquarters were surely out of their bedrolls by now, calming the tense cattle. If the herd panicked, hundreds of them might end up over in the New Mexico territory, captured by rustlers. A significant number of head might be trampled.

Suddenly, the horses jumped and reared.

"Stop." Ben tried to hang onto his own mount. What spooked them? The rough weather was still on the horizon.

And then a hot wind gust slapped him in the face.

The remuda ran.

A split second before Ben hit the ground, he saw the deathly glow. Leaping out of the south pasture was an orange wall of fire.

Dazed, he managed to regain his feet. However, his frightened mount had fled with the other horses. Though hundreds of yards away, Ben felt intense heat from the towering flames.

"Headquarters," he shouted, limping in that direction. "Laurabeth is there."

His cry was barely audible, swallowed by a roar louder than a hundred locomotives.

Ben traveled less than ten yards before his boot heel caught a prairie dog hole, twisting his injured ankle. Pain exploded the length of his leg. His head spun into dizziness, making him almost lose his supper.

Inching forward, he heard the distant bawling of crazed cattle, their frenzied cry carried atop the oven wind. A deep rumble vibrated the ground as thousands of clicking horns raced through the eerie light.

"The cattle are stampeding north," he screamed, while flaming embers shot up into the night like giant fireflies.

As Ben hobbled closer, the fire appeared to pass just east of headquarters. Even so, the scorched air became more difficult to breathe. Thick puffs of smoke gagged him, yet he made out the hands' shadowy forms. Rows of them beat out the smaller flames with wet brooms and burlap sacks. Someone wearing a bonnet and dressed in trousers offered drinking water with a bucket and dipper.

"Mrs. Landers," Ben said, yet saw no other women. "Laurabeth must be safe inside the ranch house with Cleo." He huffed a sigh of relief.

And then he spied burning cow chips riding atop a rogue wind, flying toward the ranch house.

No one else seemed to notice.

Ben attempted to scream a warning through the billowing haze, yet his lungs filled with smoke.

The ranch house roof was ablaze!

CHAPTER 25

Bong. Bong.

Chimes from the ranch house grandfather clock awoke Laurabeth from a restless sleep.

"Two o'clock in the morning," she whispered. "Where's Cleo?"

Sitting on the side of the bed, she daubed beads of perspiration with the sleeve of her gown.

Why is the room so warm?

A sudden wind gust rattled the window. Cleo must have closed the pane and drawn the curtain.

I should've told her I like the wind, even when it howls.

Laurabeth sighed as thoughts of Ben slipped into her consciousness. For some reason, her questions had upset him. Wasn't showing interest in a man's family good manners?

A strong, smoky odor halted her thoughts, reminiscent of the Galveston fire. Her pulse quickened.

"Must be a problem with the stove," she said aloud.

"Betsy?"

"Cleo?"

Laurabeth scurried into the hazy living area where a lantern brightly burned. Pieces of the dress Betsy was sewing lay on the table beside two full cups of tea. The older women were nowhere to be seen. They must have stepped out to the privy.

The haze thickened, making Laurabeth cough. "No different than the smoky orphanage kitchen," she assured herself. "The stove fire's contained. I'll adjust the damper."

The front door swung open. A scalding wind rushed into the house, blowing out the lantern.

"Betsy ... is that you?"

"Cleo?"

An eerie light filtered into the darkened room. Laurabeth's knees weakened.

"Ladies?" She faced the door.

"Is that any way to greet a male visitor who's brought you a gift?" Framed in the hellish glow was Brett Castle, the same disgusting man who forced himself on her at Colorado City. In his arms was a trunk.

"No!" Laurabeth screamed.

With a single leap, Brett dropped the trunk, seizing her in his iron grip. He slammed a soot covered hand over her mouth. "Looks like you still haven't learned the proper way to return a gentleman's kindness." He squeezed her body tighter. "Teasing up a wildfire you can't control is dangerous ... 'cept with your future husband."

Future husband?

The thought sickened her, winding the room into a lopsided spin. She attempted to struggle, but her muscles refused to cooperate. Breathing required extreme effort.

"This little present proves my sincere devotion." He released the hand from her mouth and grabbed the trunk. "Went to a lot of trouble to deliver your personal belongings."

The glow inside the room brightened. Laurabeth recognized her father's initials, then burst with indignation.

"Papa's sea chest. Don't you touch it." Managing to free a hand, she slashed fingernails across Brett's face, raising bloody stripes resembling red war paint.

"You." Her voice found an unexpected strength. "You murdered One-Eared Charlie."

Brett spit out a coarse laugh. He shoved Laurabeth to the floor, pinning her there with his boot.

The ceiling level haze thickened into black smoke.

"You've refused the final chance for a life of luxury, little girl. Payback time's arrived." He removed his gun belt as flames licked the tops of the walls. "We'll begin with a kiss, then see where that leads."

Laurabeth fought with all of her remaining strength. "I'll burn before you steal from me again."

Boom!

Thunder clapped as Ben flew through the door, tackling Brett from behind. Both men crashed against a chair.

"Ben. Get out. The roof's on fire." Laurabeth reached for him, but the suffocating heat made her dizzy.

In an instant, Brett was back on his feet. Ben stood as well, yet Brett knocked the boy onto the table with a single blow. A hard kick to the stomach left Ben gasping for air.

"I'm gonna do you a favor, son." Brett spoke beneath wild eyes. "So you won't be around to watch the fun I have in mind for her." Pulling El Cuchillo's long knife from a boot, Brett lunged forward.

"Watch out," Laurabeth screamed. "Ben."

Regaining breath, Ben rolled. Brett missed his target, plunging the knife deep into the wood. While attempting to withdraw the blade, a single ceiling timber snapped and fell.

Brett lay motionless on the floor.

Rushing to Laurabeth, Ben scooped her into his arms, then limped to the door.

Crazed laughter erupted from behind. Laurabeth turned her head to see Brett up on one knee, his pistol pointed at Ben's back.

Boom!

A deafening thunderclap.

Followed by a tremendous crack.

The ranch house roof collapsed in a shower of sparks and massive burning timbers, this time burying Brett.

More thunder covered Laurabeth's scream.

Outside, Ben carried her to a safe distance.

Refusing to let go of him, she dissolved into his protective embrace.

"Are you all right?"

She tried to answer but coughed.

"I'll go and fetch water."

Laurabeth coughed again. "No. Please." She cleared her throat. "Don't leave me."

He drew her closer.

A brief image of Brett Castle pushed into her memory, followed by a replay of the ranch house roof collapse and his certain demise.

How dare he steal her papa's sea chest.

She shivered.

The precious Appleby family items saved from one fire were now destroyed by another.

Then Ben's voice interrupted her thoughts. "I owe you my life. I ... I'm so sorry about—"

Laurabeth repositioned herself to face him, shushing a finger over his mouth.

Ben gently brushed her hand aside, lacing his fingers with hers. "Please, there's only minutes before the others arrive."

He glanced up at the burning ranch house, then back toward her. "I never knew my real folks. My father was an outlaw, my mother ... I was a baby when she left."

Laurabeth's mind spun. *That's why he'd gone silent when she'd compared him to his parents.*

He continued. "Some folks adopted me but never treated me as a child of their own." Ben swallowed. "So I found God."

She spoke at a whisper. "That's why you're my shooting star."

"And the reason you're mine." Drawing her closer than before, Ben looked deeply into her eyes, then pressed his lips against hers.

Brilliant splinters of light danced across the western sky. They remained alone only seconds longer before everyone was there, talking all at once and asking what happened. A minute later, Useless appeared, blabbering how his mules had warned him to return early.

Laurabeth continued to gaze into Ben's clear blue eyes as steady raindrops blended with her tears.

CHAPTER 26

A misty dawn revealed the only structure destroyed in the fire was the ranch house. The outbuildings suffered slight smoke damage, while the chuckwagon and yellow buck-buggy remained unharmed.

Wrapped in a blanket, Laurabeth sat beside the campfire. Cleo—still wearing her elaborate hat—poured fresh coffee, enlightening Cookie about the brew's medicinal benefits. "The stronger the better." She slurped an enormous gulp.

Laurabeth stared at the ranch house's charred remains, then glanced skyward at a layer of thick grey clouds. Cookie had rustled her up some dry clothes, while Cleo insisted upon the blanket.

"Looks like more beneficial rain's on tap." Betsy handed Laurabeth a steaming cup, then whispered. "Too bad we're not sipping my mellow tea."

"I'm sorry about your home. All the beautiful things." Laurabeth noticed the singed cuffs of her new friend's trousers.

Betsy smiled, her face smudged with soot. "When I married George, I knew prairie fires came with the territory. My cast iron stove is fine of course. Everything else surrendered to the blaze."

Sipping the hot liquid, Laurabeth considered Betsy's words. The same brand of *territory* was attached to Ben Diamond. The thought made her heart flutter. He'd saved her life, and then kissed her.

Kissed her.

Standing in the rain, he'd surrounded her with his gentle strength, releasing a secret piece of his heart. Then while gazing into her eyes, he'd pressed his lips against hers.

Seconds later, her emotions spilled. She wept tears of joy and relief mixed with compassion and remembrance. Laurabeth wasn't sure how long he'd held her after the others arrived. When she'd finally whispered *I'm all right*, he'd squeezed her hand, tipped his soggy hat, and limped away to find the herd.

How could such a tender moment reside on the edge of one so tragic.

The creak of wagon wheels announced the arrival of Useless, Colt, and Mr. Landers. They'd driven out to bury Brett and survey the burn damage.

Useless sniffed the air. "Nothing beats the aroma of Cookie's boiling branch water."

Cookie poured three cups. "Miss Cleopatra says my coffee's got healing powers."

"Makes sense to me." Useless sniffed his cup. "This concoction could pass as first-rate castor oil."

Cleo hooted. "You two scoundrels keep my giggle box active. Truth is, Daddy swore strong coffee mends an ailing back. Ain't that right, little brother?"

"Daddy swore."

"How many head were lost?" Cookie asked.

"'Bout a dozen." Mr. Landers took a satisfied sip. "The boys are close to having the herd collected."

Betsy joined her husband. "What about the fire?"

The foreman cocked his hat. "South pasture took a huge hit. Rain saved the rest. We were lucky."

Useless grinned. "Mister and Mizz keep predicting the drought's over."

"If them mules ain't fibbing," Cleo bellowed, "I'll kiss 'em both."

Everyone laughed.

"I'm stunned the Castle boy murdered One-Eared Charlie," Betsy said. "His father is such a fine man. I suppose Brett set the fire too?"

"My guess is that the flames were a diversion so he could get to Miss Appleby." Mr. Landers glanced in Laurabeth's direction. "But the blaze was ignited by one of our own men. Fellow named Jake Crow."

"Ain't no surprise he's the culprit." Cookie patted his apron, releasing a puff of flour. "Never did like that scamp, Crow. Ought to be horsewhipped and jailed."

"Boy's dead." The boss wore a grim expression. "Got stomped to death by a mustang. Found his body in the south pasture where the fire started. There were matches and an empty whisky bottle beside him. Exactly why he was in cahoots with Castle is anybody's guess."

"A horse killed him?" Laurabeth stood. "Did the remuda run in that direction?"

Landers scratched his head. "That's the mystery. The remuda stampeded north with the cattle. This animal acted alone. Tracks come out of that hidden offshoot in Yellow House Canyon."

"Where are the horses now?" Laurabeth asked.

"Headed this way. I've ordered them taken west of here to graze." The foreman grinned. "And that cowboy who saved your life—"

"Ben Diamond," Cleo blurted.

"I told Diamond early this morning he'd been promoted to an official hand. Though he'll stay on as wrangler till I can hire someone else."

"I owe a debt of gratitude to that boy." Useless stepped toward his wagon.

"Looks like I'm back to gathering prairie coal." Cookie pooched out his lower lip.

Everyone laughed again.

Rejoining the group, Useless faced his niece. "Discovered this earlier while poking through the ranch house rubble." From behind his back, he produced a small trunk.

"Papa's sea chest. I thought it was destroyed when the roof collapsed."

Her uncle winked. "Rain must've saved it. Outside's a little scorched, but I'll bet the inside's fine."

Laurabeth took the trunk and gently set it on the ground. Trembling, she opened the latch. Inside were the Appleby family Bible, her father's pipe, and mother's wedding gown. All three items remained in good condition.

"I'd like for you to have this." She handed her uncle the pipe.

"Well, Missy. Reckon such a device would look better hanging from my jaw than yours." He paused, examining the hand carved detail. "I'll smoke it while we freight around this here XIT Ranch together."

Laurabeth flung her arms around him. For once, he had nothing to say.

"Now ain't that sweet." Cleo wiped her eyes with the hem of her skirt.

In the distance, the remuda rumbled into view at a rapid clip. As Laurabeth searched for Ben, she glimpsed the beautiful blue stallion emerge from the middle.

The majestic creature reared up on his hind legs before disappearing back into the herd.

"Haven't seen that animal before," Landers said.

As the rest of the group discussed the remuda's latest addition, Laurabeth eyed Ben. He rode in total command, proud and tall, atop the golden mare. Turning his head in Laurabeth's direction, he grinned, waving his hat until the herd passed out of sight.

"Did I ever tell y'all about the time Mister, Mizz, and me run across a polka-dotted mule?"

Laurabeth didn't hear the rest of her uncle's story. Reaching into the trunk, she removed the lacy wedding gown. Then stroking the rich fabric, she was lost once again in recollection of Ben's deep blue eyes.

Felt the tenderness of his strong embrace.

Remembered the depth of his newfound faith.

Thank you, Heavenly Father, that he's my shooting star ... and I'm his.

Clutching the gown next to her heart, a tear of pure joy slid down her cheek. Her self-made promise of finding *genuine happiness* wasn't broken.

An intuitive tingle coursed the full length of her spine.

For one day soon, she'd wear the lovely gown.

And his lips would melt into hers.

Then together as one ...

They'd travel over the horizon.

The End

ABOUT THE AUTHOR

Timothy Lewis is the author of *The Glitter Effect*, a middle grade mystery released by Elk Lake Publishing, Inc. as well as *Running Downwind*. He's also the author of *Forever Friday*, released in September of 2013 by Waterbrook Press, and translated into multiple languages. The novel's been featured four times in *Reader's Digest Select Editions*. He's only the second *Reader's Digest* author of an inspirational crossover title in over twenty-five years. Reviewers on BookBub, Goodreads, Barnes & Noble, and Amazon have compared his poetic prose to Nicholas Sparks. In an article for *USA Today*, a former Waterbrook editor likened him to Garrison Keillor.

TIMOTHY LEWIS

A published playwright, he's penned more than twenty plays/musicals and over a hundred songs. His article, "Freighting on the XIT Ranch of Texas," was published in the *Panhandle-Plains Historical Review*. He's also the cofounder of the West Texas Writers' Academy, which was held annually at West Texas A&M University for over a decade.

Timothy has a bachelor's degree in Music Education (BMED) from Sam Houston State University, and has studied master's level playwrighting at The University of Texas. He's also a graduate of The Institute of Children's Literature.

www.ingramcontent.com/pod-product-compliance
Lightning Source LLC
Chambersburg PA
CBHW051136020726
47501CB00005B/1541